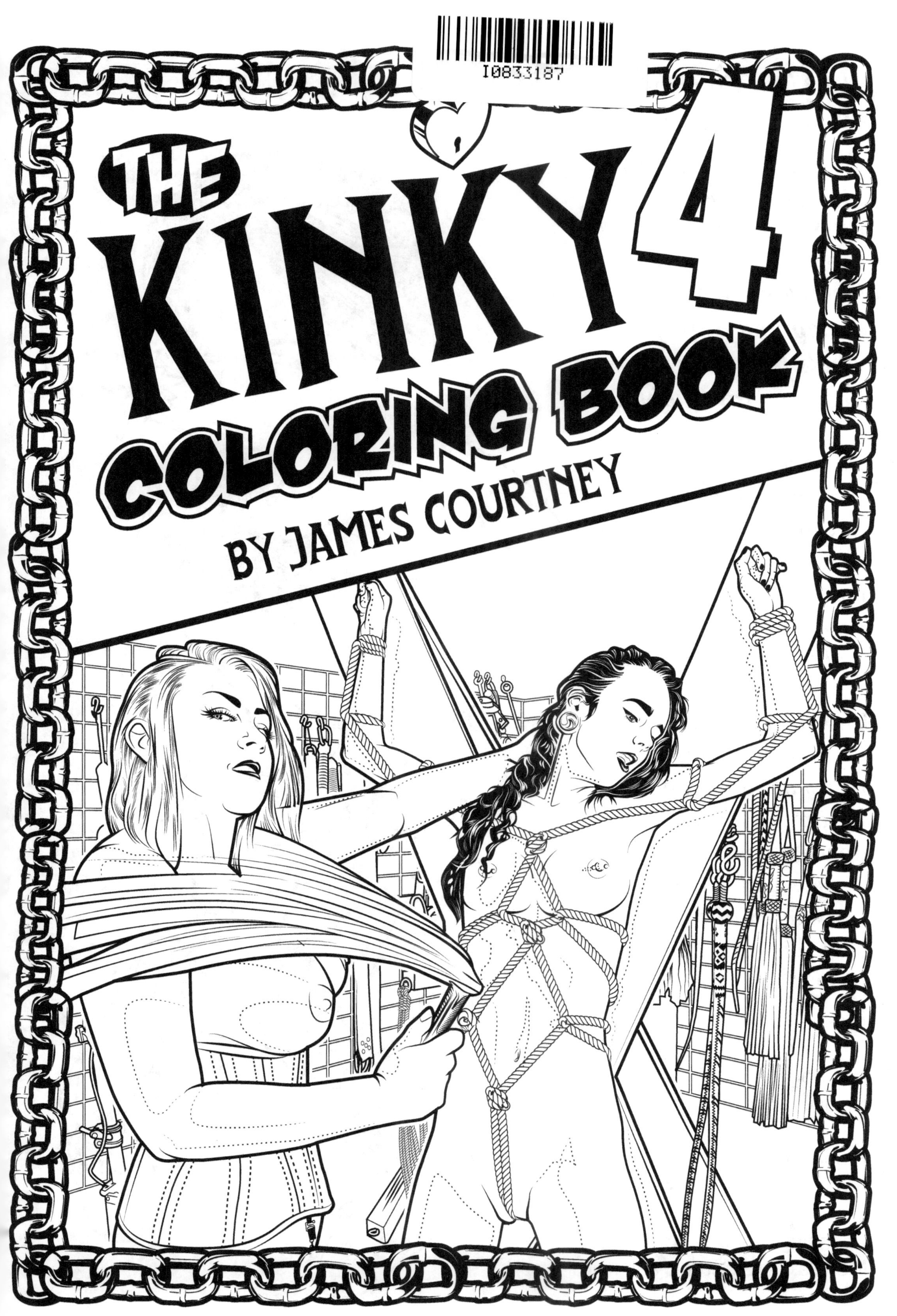
I0833187
THE
KINKY 4
COLORING BOOK
BY JAMES COURTNEY

The Kinky Coloring Book 4
By James Courtney

ISBN 978-0-9858999-3-6

Dedicated to Mariah Carle carlephotography.com who's help over the years has been invaluable.

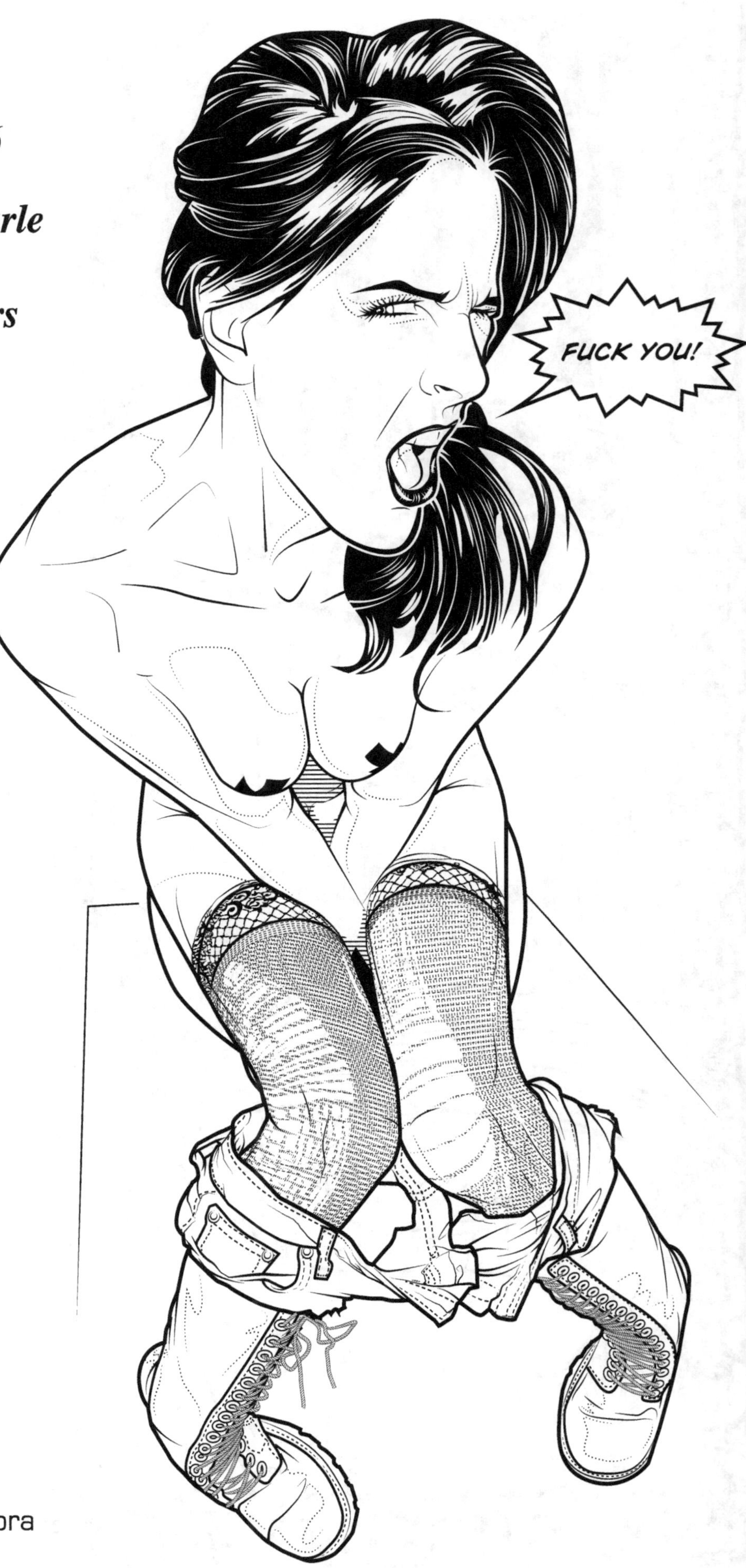

Left Page,
Model: Tia Leigh

Front Cover,
Model: Chelsea Christian

Openning Page:
Models: Kara Catonic and Aurora

Congratulations on your purchase of the Kinky Coloring Book 4 (unless you stole it, in which case shame on you!) Since you have already given me your hard-earned money, feel free to skip this introduction and get right to coloring. If, on the other hand, you are just leafing through the book and wondering if you should shell out the cover price to buy it, please read on and I will tell you about the wonders that await you within these pages.

A lot has been written this past year concerning the benefits of coloring books for adults. For example, studies show that coloring promotes a sense of calm and mindfulness. As a result, the bulk of coloring books for adults seem to be mostly collections of mandalas, geometric patterns, flowers, plants, and animals. In my humble opinion, these illustrations have no grander purpose other than to give you a series of line drawings to color in. Only the level of complexity of the drawings seem to separate them from regular children's coloring books.

There are also a few other "Adult" coloring books out there that include more R-rated themes. Sadly, many of these use art that appears rudimentary, simplistic, and not as satisfying to look at, let alone color. For coloring books with adult subject matter, your choices have been limited, but you deserve more! Your sanity and creativity begs for more options, and I'm going to give them to you.

Therefore, the goal of the Kinky Coloring Books is to give you adult themed coloring books with beautiful and intricate drawings to color.

This fourth edition of the collection represents my best efforts yet. Along with some familiar faces from the previous editions, I've also worked with some new models in this book, including Kara Catonic, Aurora, Tia Leigh, and others. I also feel that my sense of what makes for a good coloring book illustration has improved with each edition. The irony of drawing for coloring books is that the piece is never really actualized until you (the buyer) colors it. Thus, my purpose as an artist is to give you eye-catching and tantalizing imagery to look at while you color.

One of the great joys of being an artist is when you can lose yourself working on something challenging and captivating. I hope that coloring the images in this book allow you a chance to experience that for yourself.

So please, buy this book! Take it home and enjoy coloring the wonderful models within. Really, YOU are the artist here! You can achieve calm mindfulness coloring boobies just as well as geometric patterns. Life is too short to waste on mandalas. Give it a try. After all, there are far too few adult pleasures these days that don't end in either rehab or jail.

James Courtney

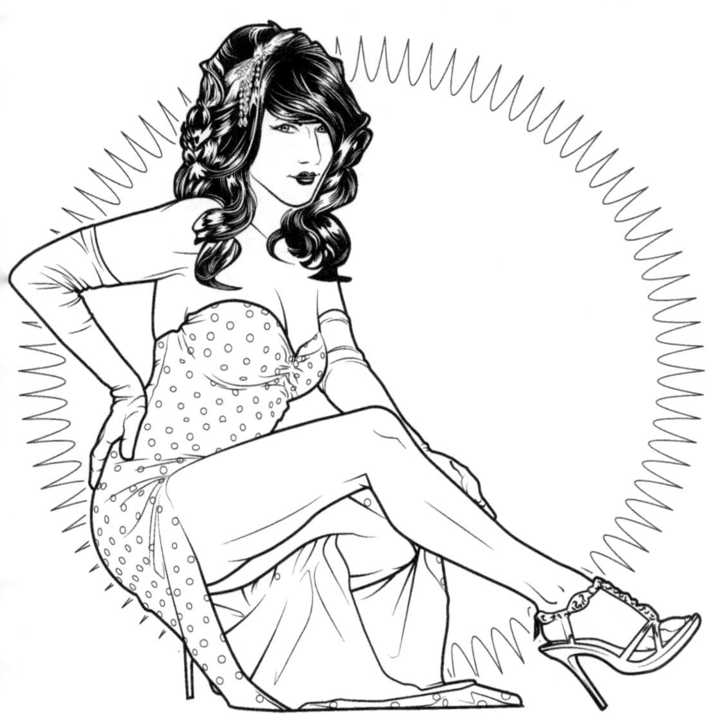

Model: Lillie De Luna
From a reference photo by
Chelsea Christian

Before they were sold in comic book shops, most comics were sold on news racks and stands in stores. As a result, the covers would have a fairly uniform format, so people could see the title of each one clearly as they were stacked in rows. Every summer, many comics would do an "annual" edition, which is a double-sized book featuring a longer story and extra content. I decided to base the design of this drawing on the Marvel Annuals of the 1970's.

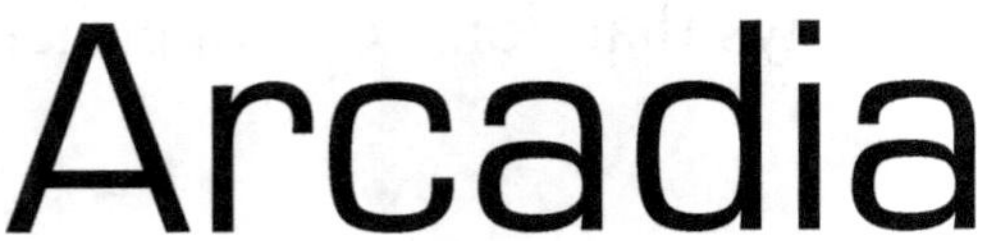

Arcadia

Model: Arcadia Kane

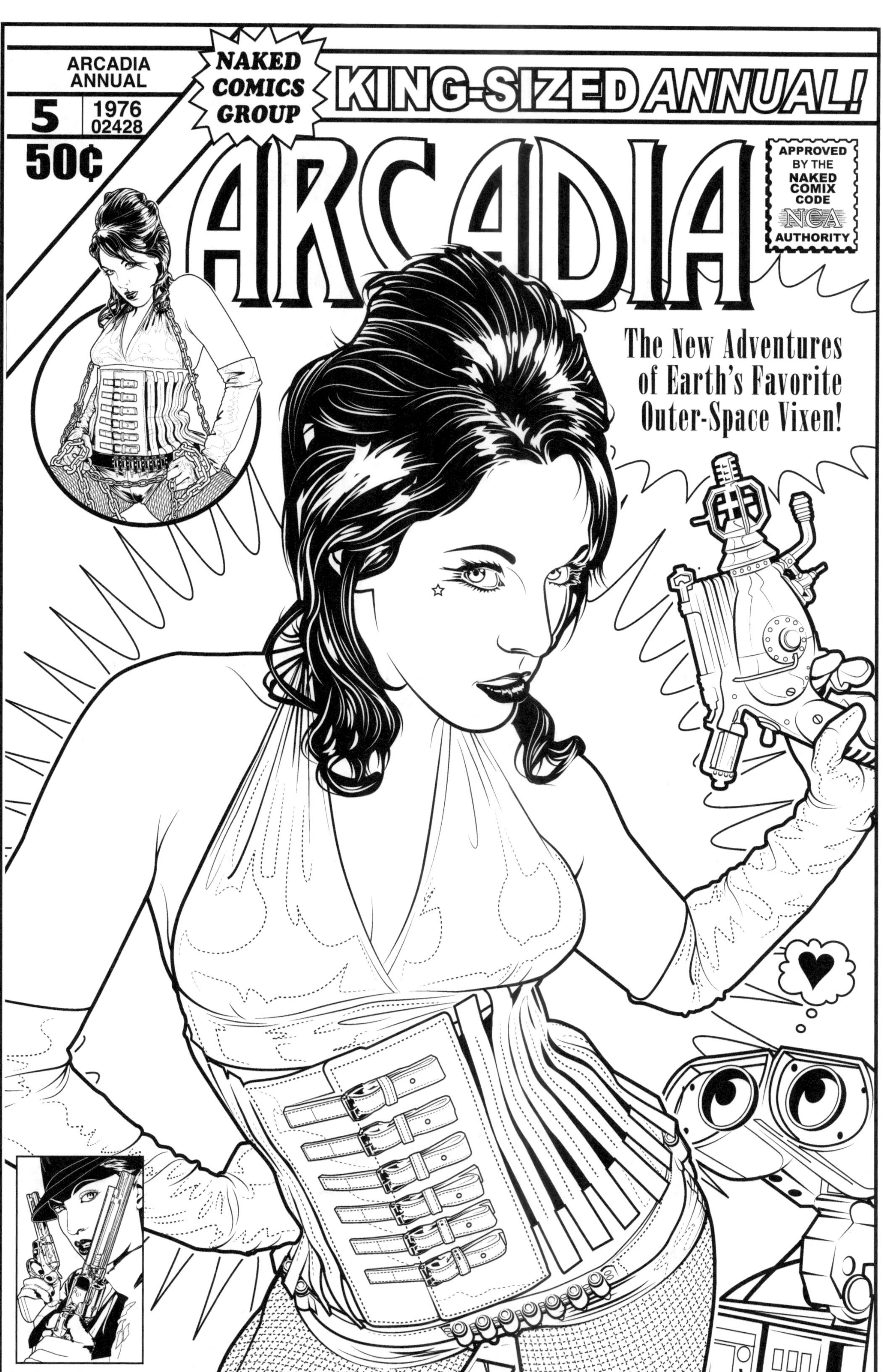
ARCADIA
ANNUAL
5
1976
02428
50¢
NAKED
COMICS
GROUP
KING-SIZED ANNUAL!
ARCADIA
APPROVED
BY THE
NAKED
COMIX
CODE
NCA
AUTHORITY
The New Adventures
of Earth's Favorite
Outer-Space Vixen!

In the story of Frankenstein, (and in many other science fiction tales), one of the major themes is the fear of not being able to control the things we create. This theme has been carried on in modern works with Terminator, The Matrix, and others, all of which showcasing the fear of the things we create turning on us. The rise of the perverted sex robots is my contribution to this thematic literary legacy.

Back In The Lab...

Models: Maggie and Ned Mayhem

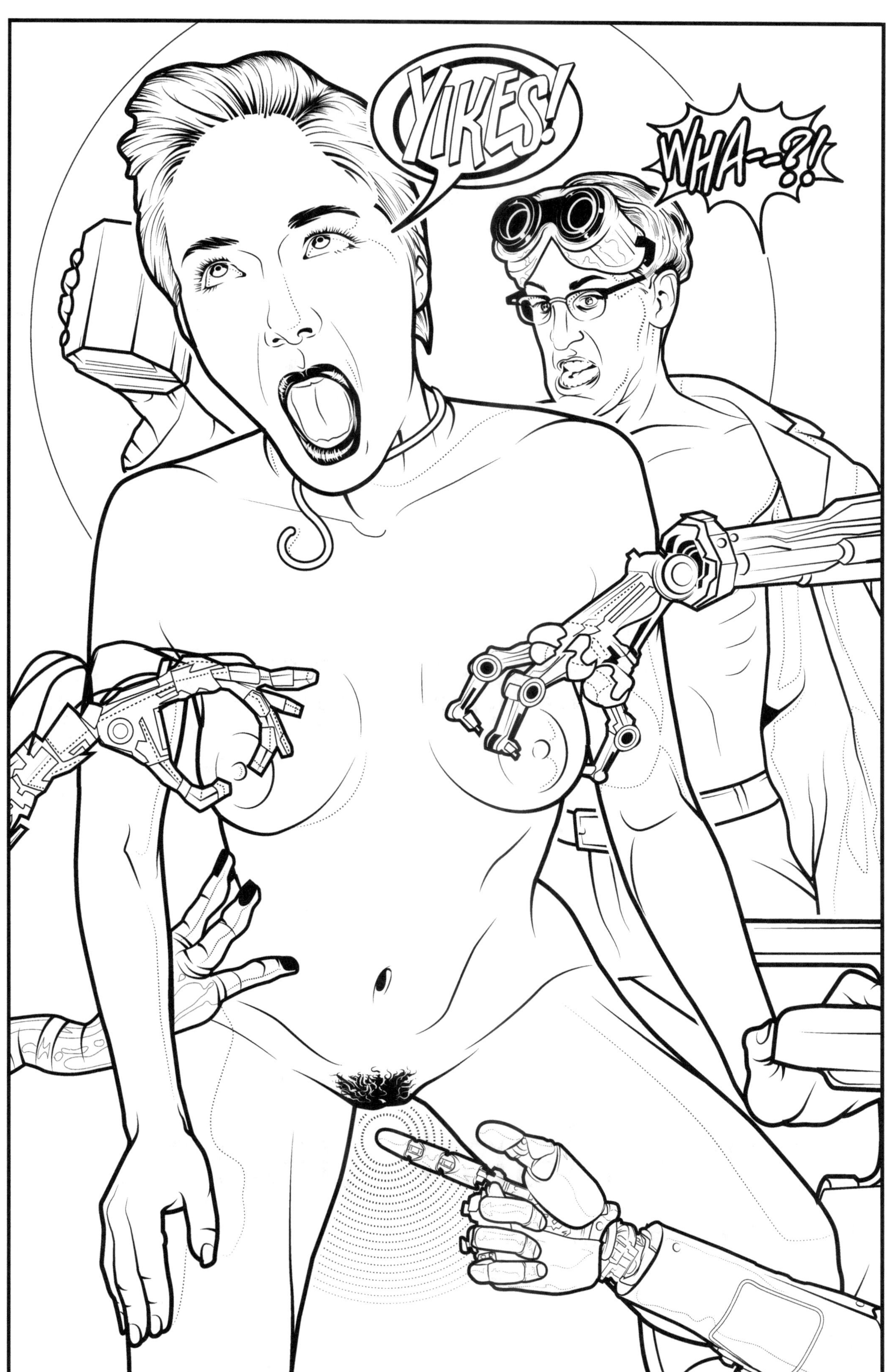
YIKES!
WHA--?!

Kara is actually a very nice girl, but every once in awhile she happens to enjoy participating in a good Viking raid.

Barbarian Queen

Model: Kara Catonic

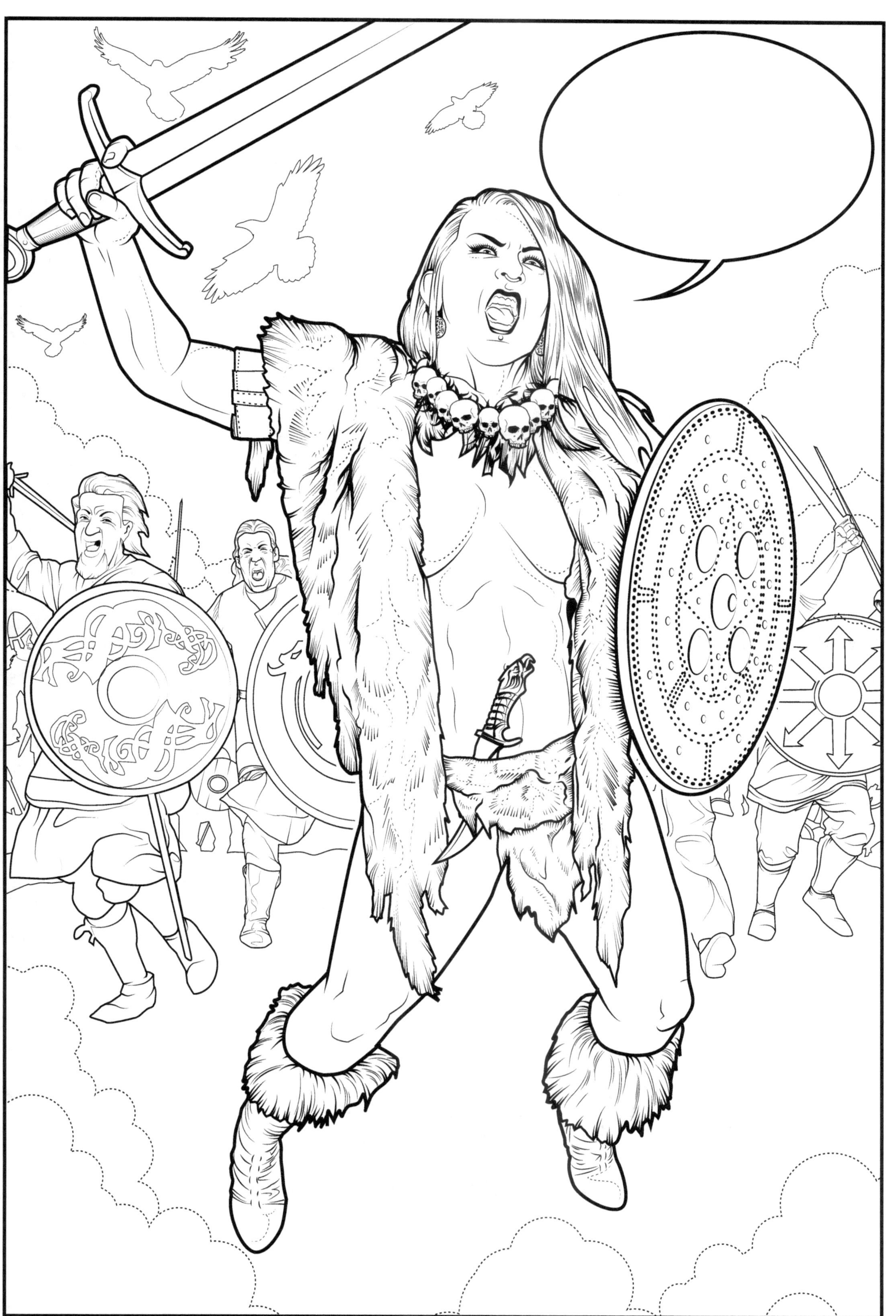

I wouldn't think of doing a coloring book without Penny in it!

Bombshells

Model: Penny McClish, Outfit by Lust Designs

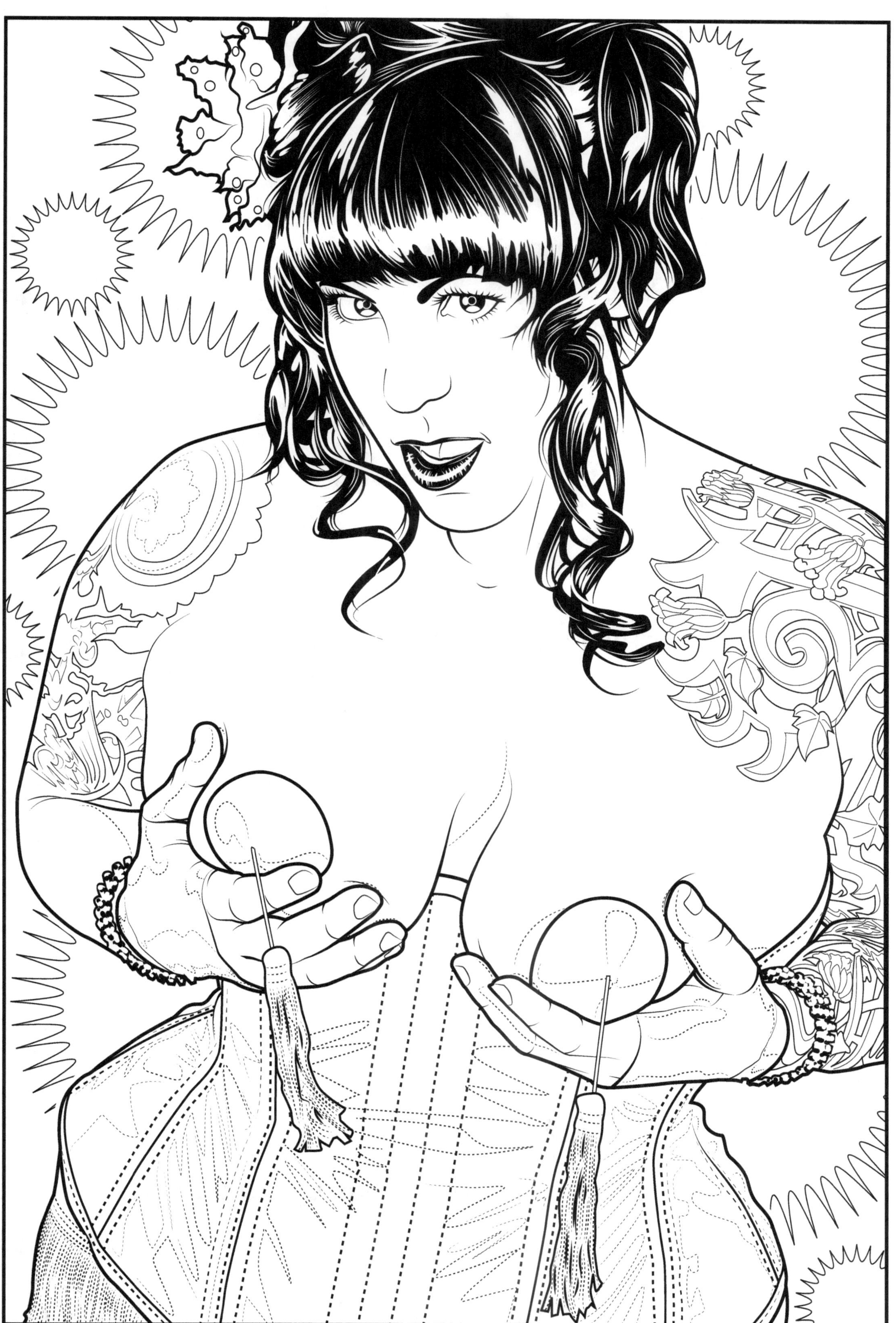

This is from my first photo shoot of the year. There is something comforting about being able to create art from new points of reference. It means I'm covering fresh ground instead of just living off of past glories.

Cleaning

Model: Chelsea Christian, Latex Dress by Lust Designs

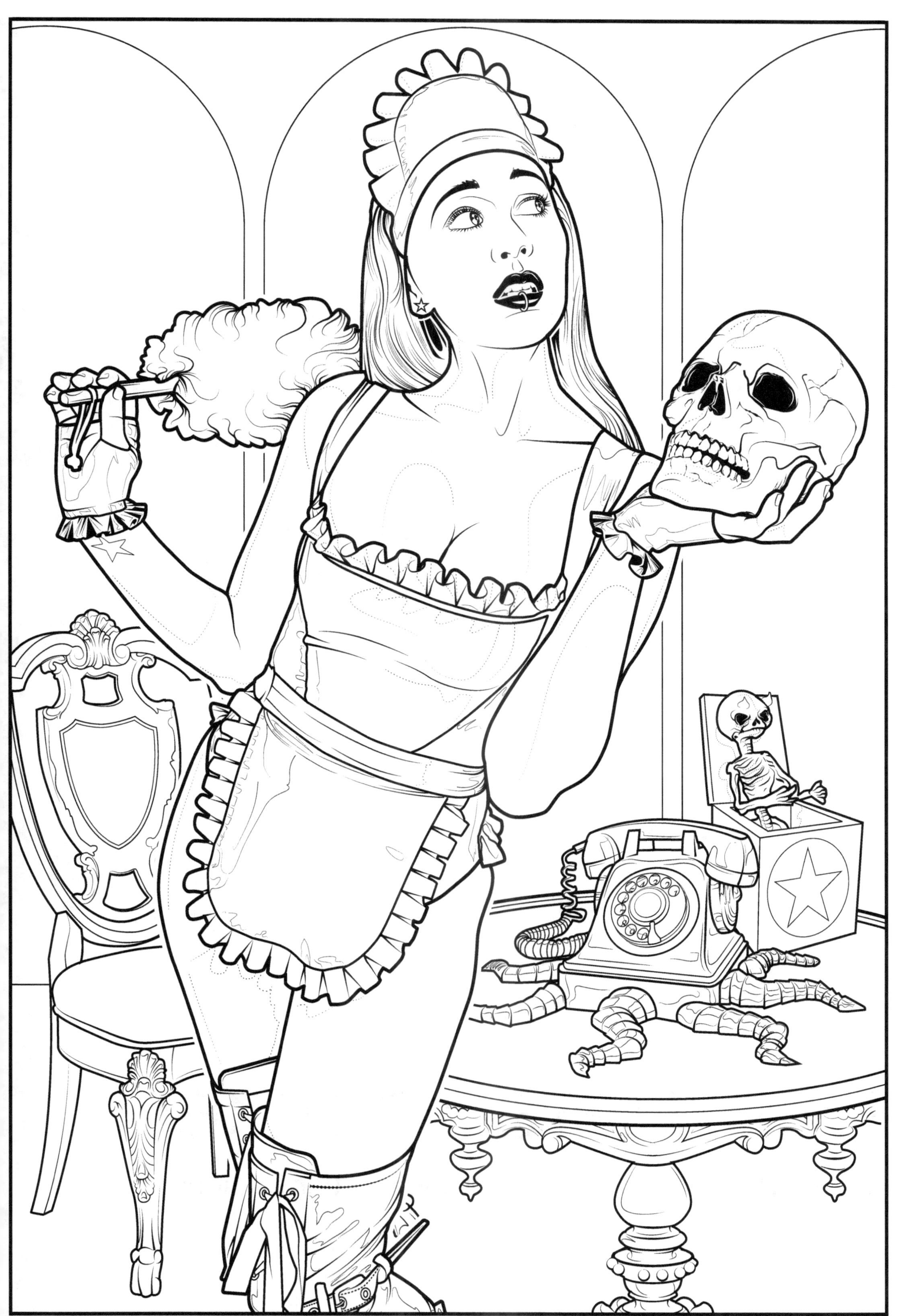

It's tough being a working mother.

Dani Gets Spanked

Model: Dani Red, Spanking Dress by Lust Designs

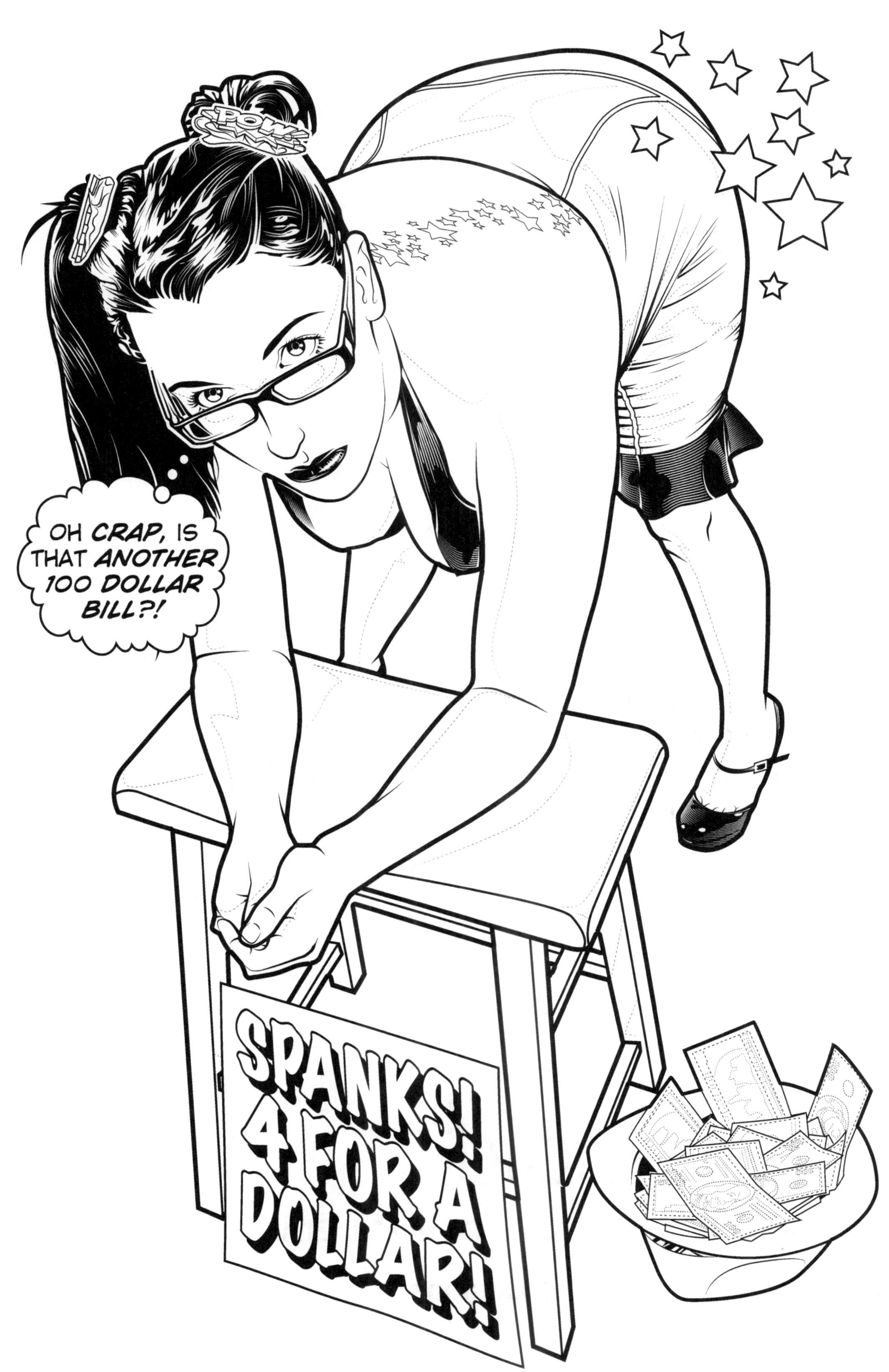
POW
OH CRAP, IS THAT ANOTHER 100 DOLLAR BILL?!
SPANKS! 4 FOR A DOLLAR!

I wanted one illustration of Penny and Jeff together in this edition, so I asked Penny to put one of her roller derby moves on Jeff. I wasn't too worried about the boy. Penny knows just how much pressure to put on a man, and Jeff is tough enough to take it.

Chokehold

Models: Jeff Cathcart and Penny McClish

Outfit designed by Lust Designs

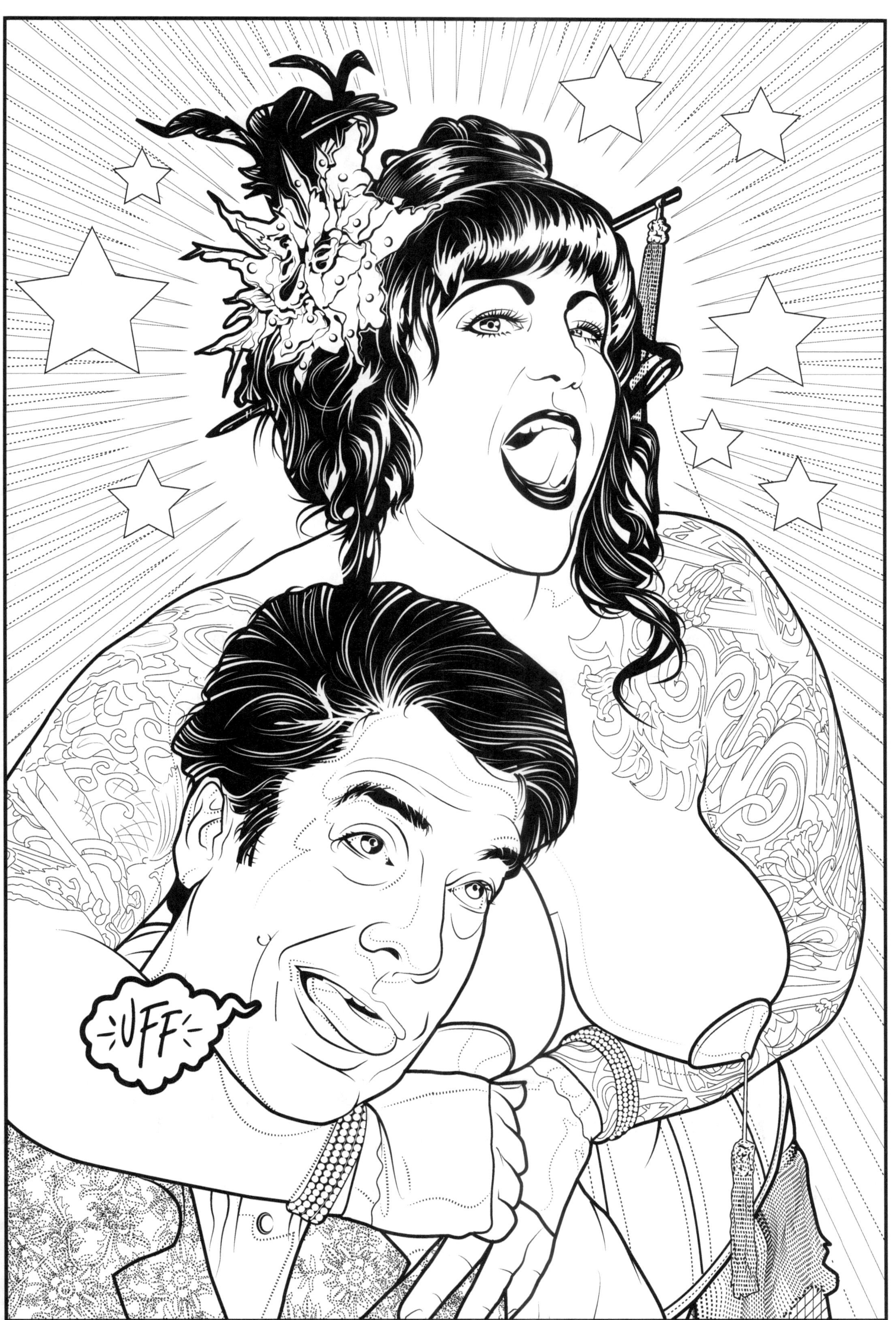
UFF

One of the dangers of shooting models in your own home is they eventually check out what you have in the refrigerator.

Daisy In The Kitchen

Model: Daisy Night

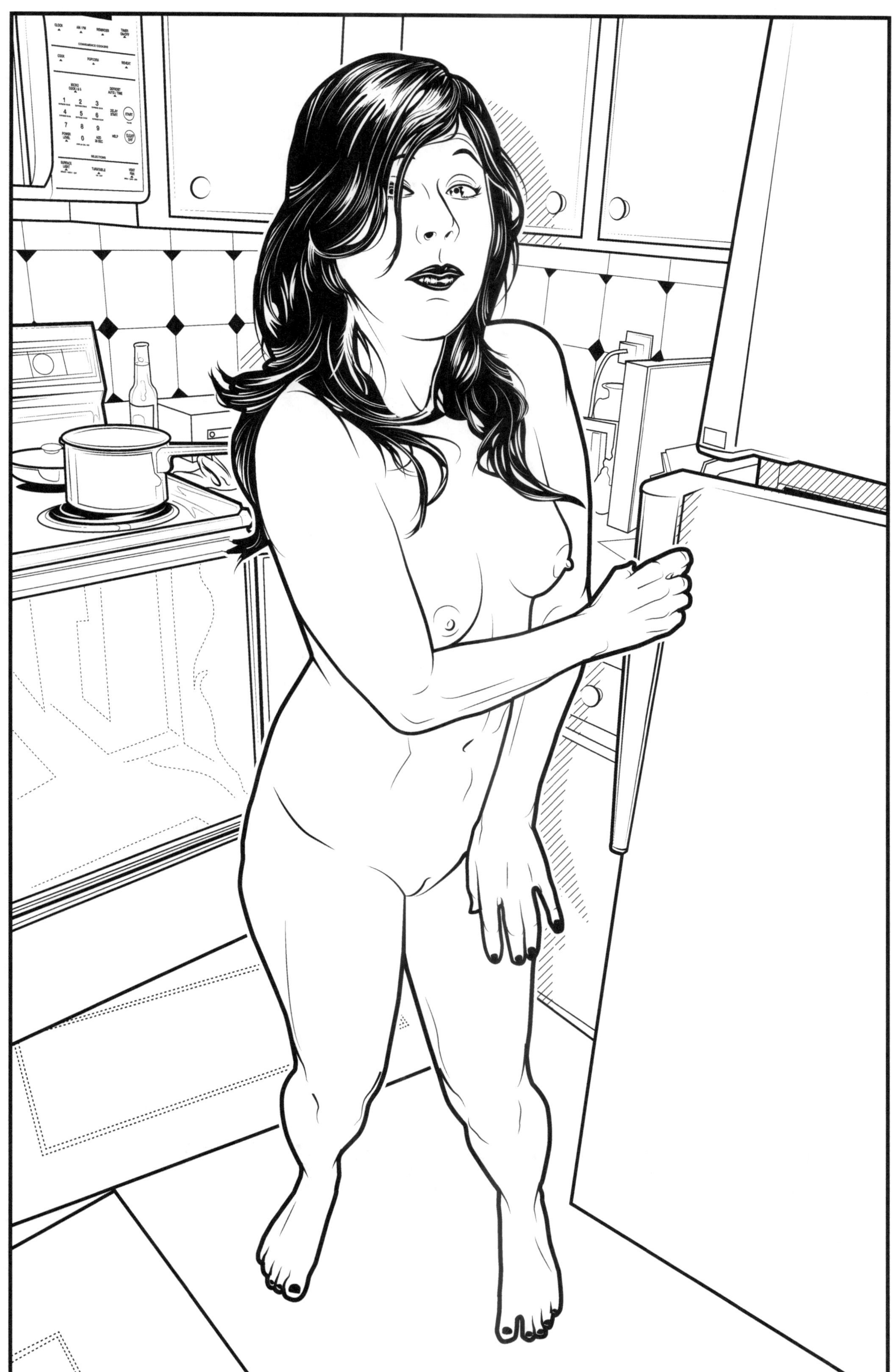
CLOCK
AM / PM
REMINDER
TIMER ON/OFF
CONVENIENCE COOKING
COOK
POPCORN
REHEAT
MICRO COOK I & II
DEFROST AUTO / TIME
1
2
3
4
5
6
DELAY START
START
7
8
9
POWER LEVEL
0
ADD 30 SEC
HELP
CLEAR OFF
SELECTIONS
SURFACE LIGHT
TURNTABLE
VENT FAN

"I'm really a terrible person who hides it well."
–Chelsea

Deadman's Party

Model: Chelsea Christian

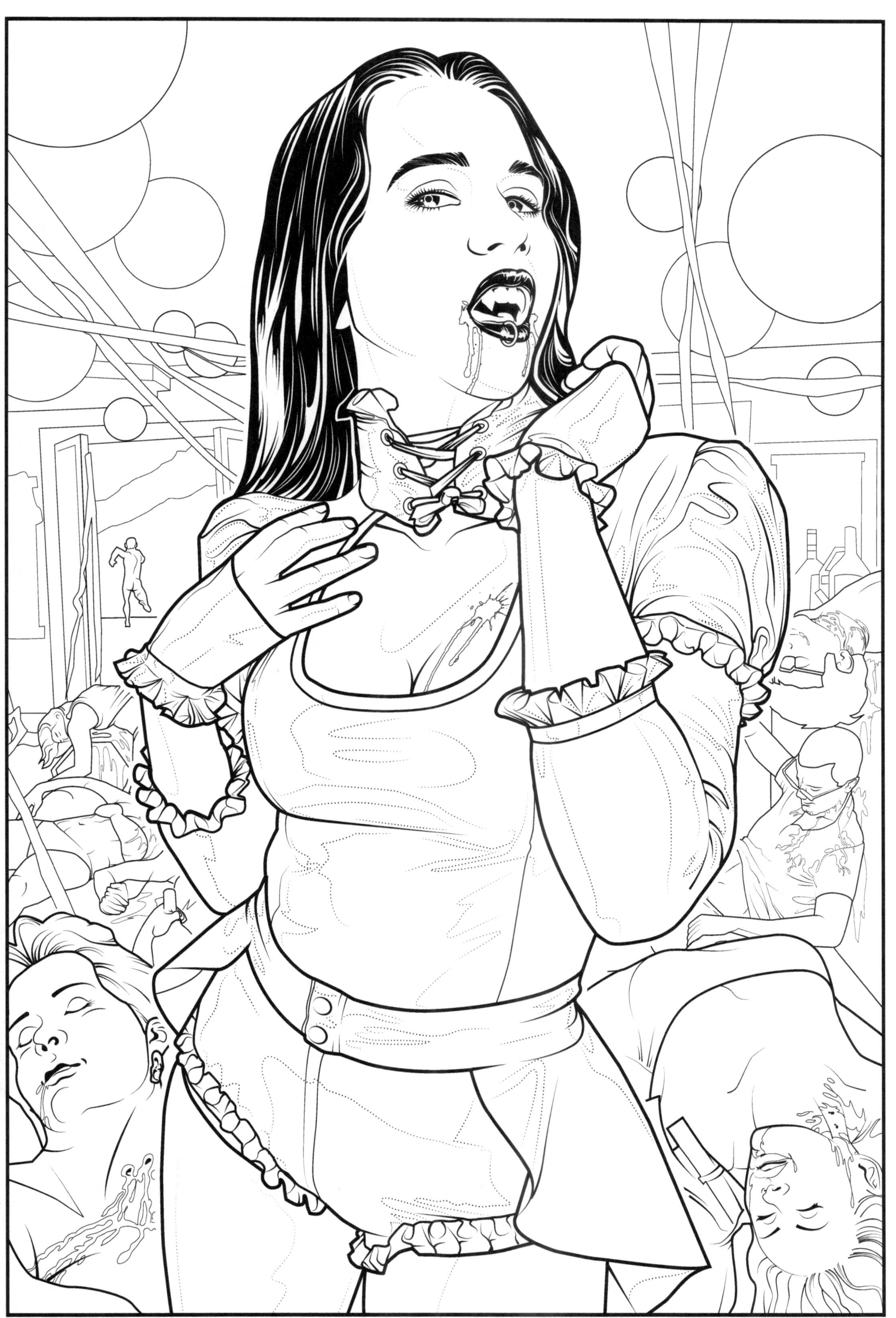

Penny dresses up for a night of Ultra-Violence with her Droogs before returning home for a glass of Drencrom and a bit of the Ludwig Van.

Clockwork Penny

Models: Penny McClish, Droog Outfit by Lust Designs

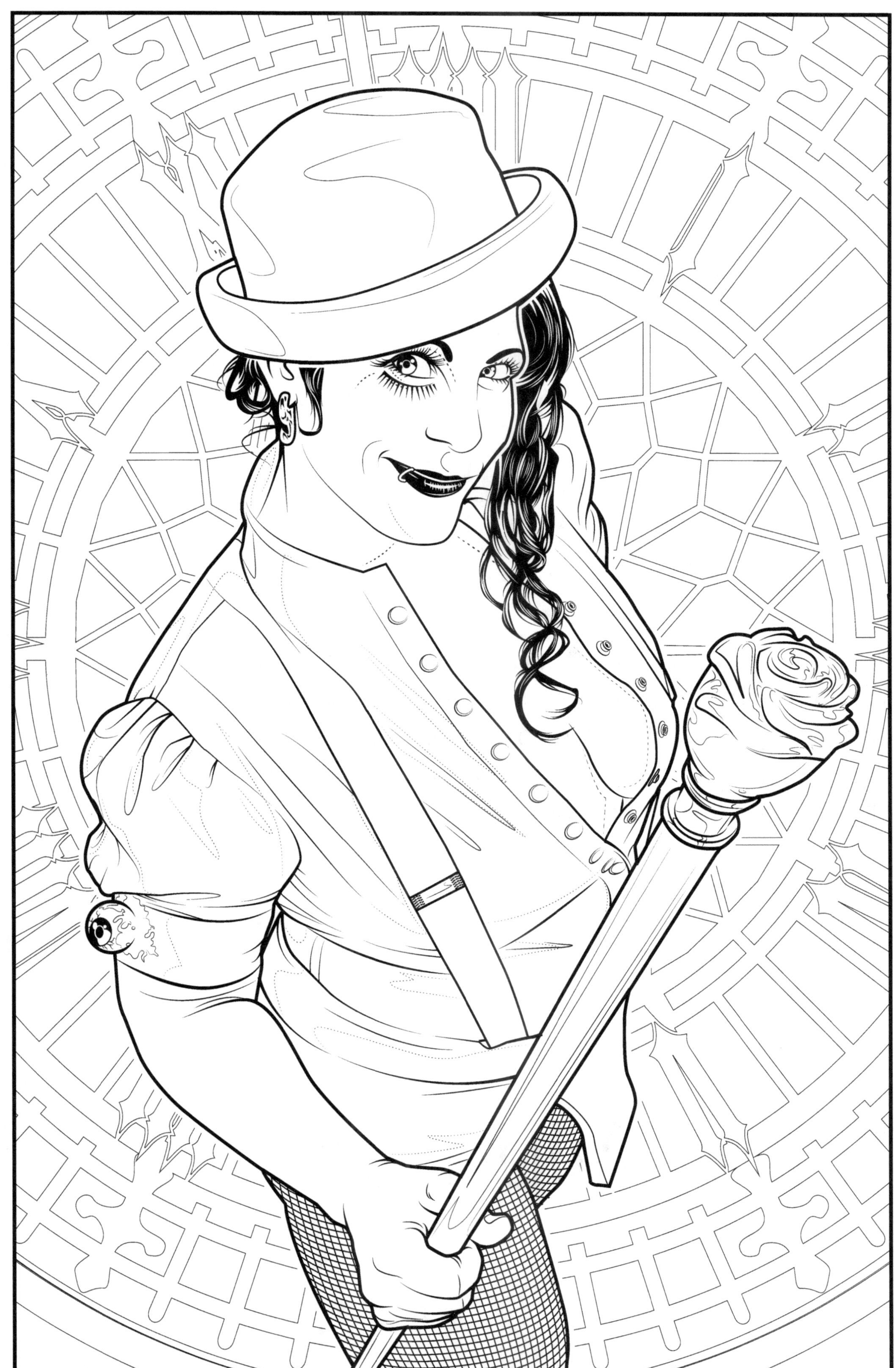

I took the reference photograph for this illustration only a month or so before Dani gave birth to her son. At one point, he started kicking in the middle of the photoshoot. I guess he wanted us all to know that he was still in the picture.

Earth Mother

Model: Dani Red

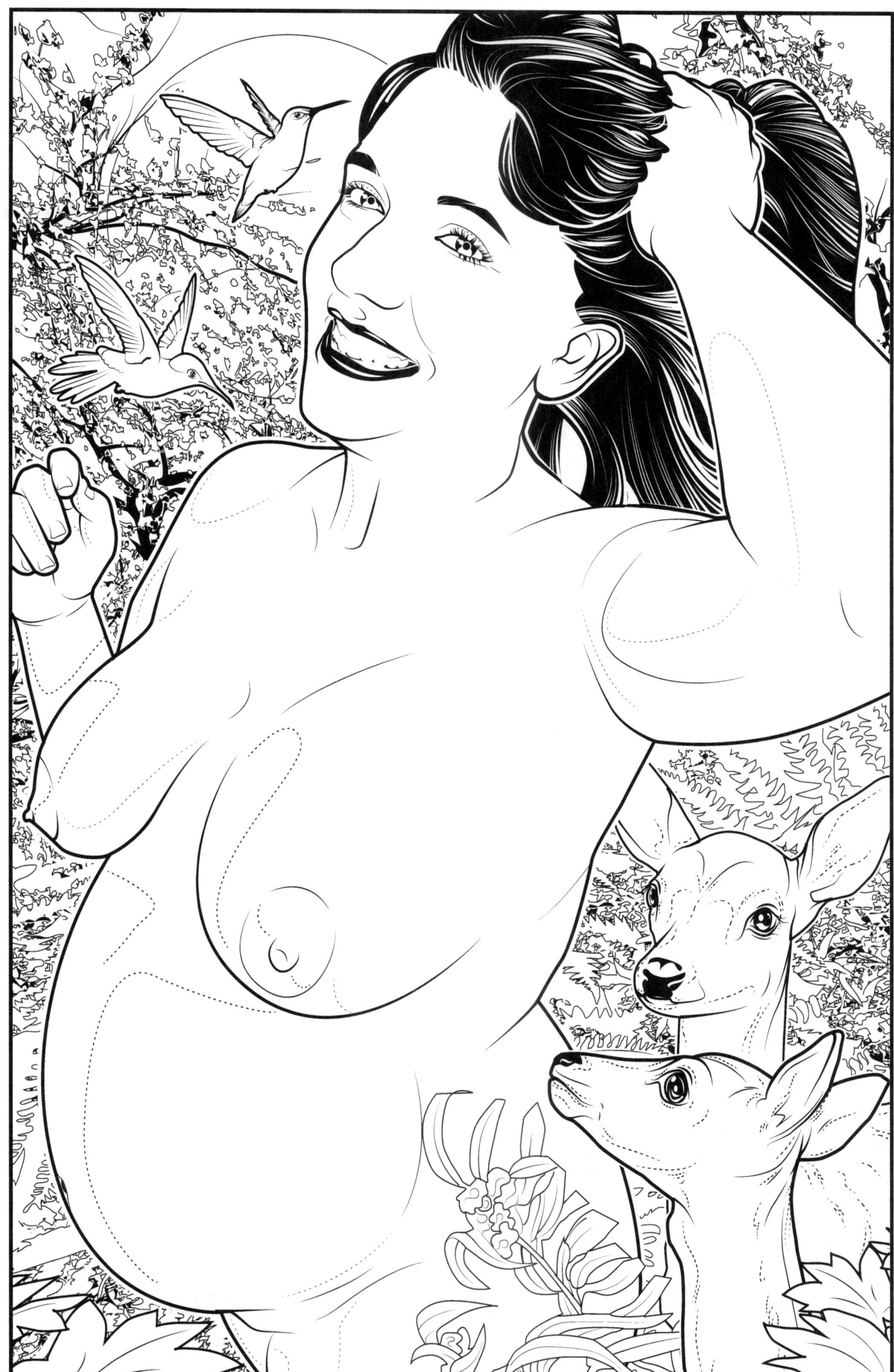

Here is Freakymar5 digging her evil claws deep into a helpless victim. If you are lucky, she may do it to you next!

Evil Grab

Models: WunderPanties & Freakymar5,

Chain Rigging: CorruptMorals, Make-Up: HisDame

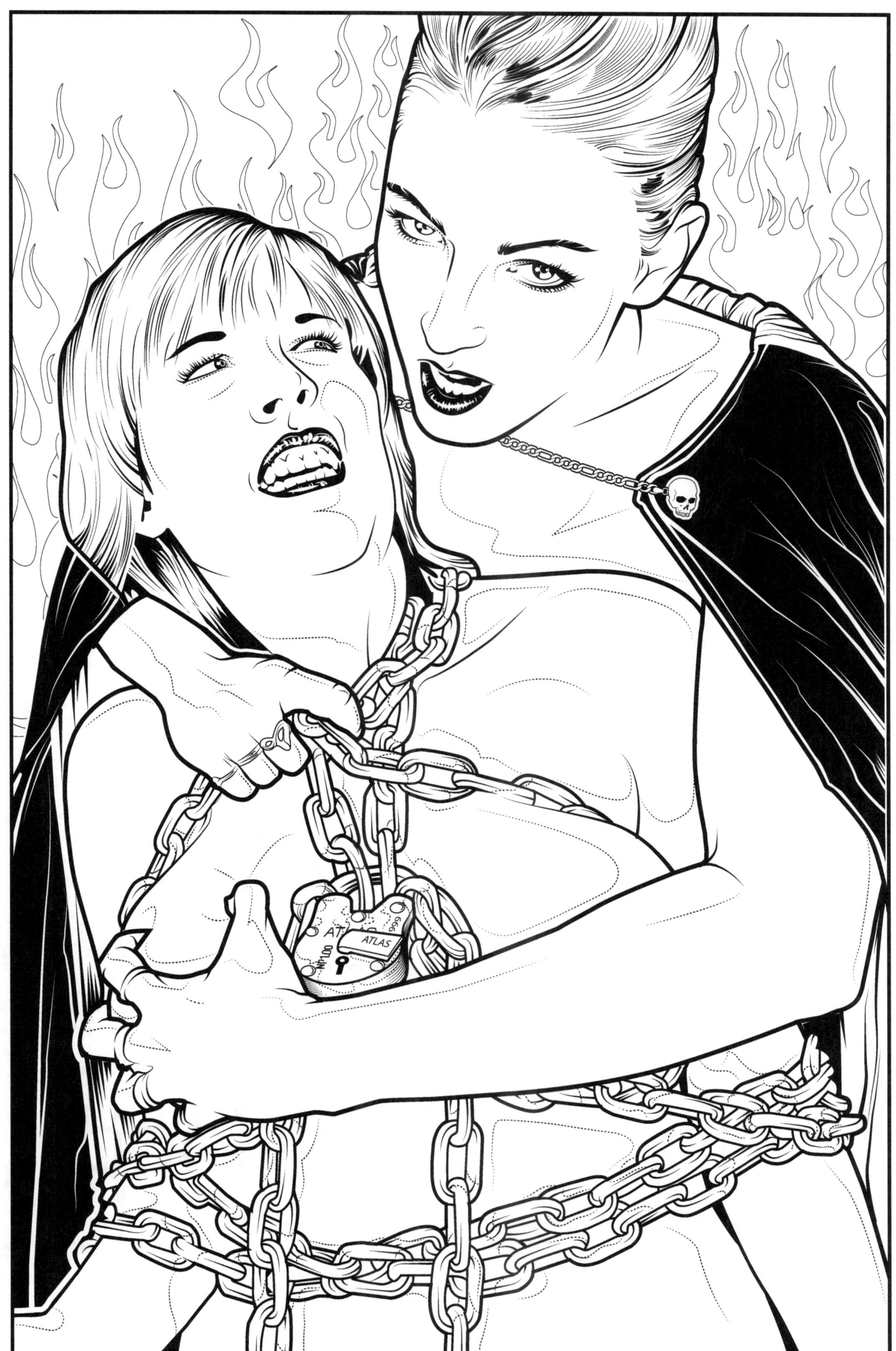
ATLAS

Pooh Bear is going to be so pissed when he finds out that somebody else has been getting into his honey!

Finger Licking Good

Models: Kara Catonic

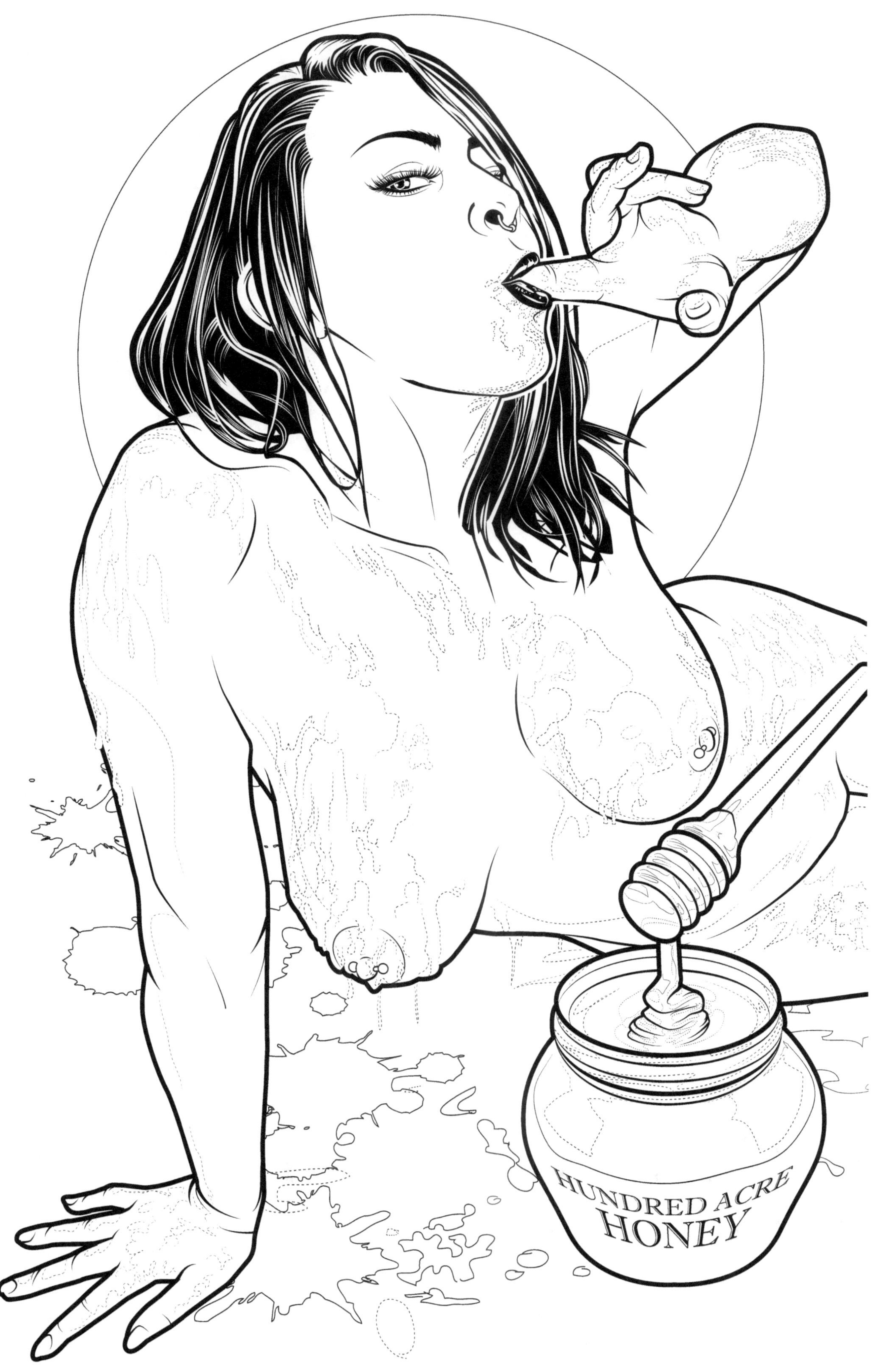
HUNDRED ACRE
HONEY

Davina finds a grey hare, but she doesn't seem to care!

Fuzzy Animals

Model: Davina Darling

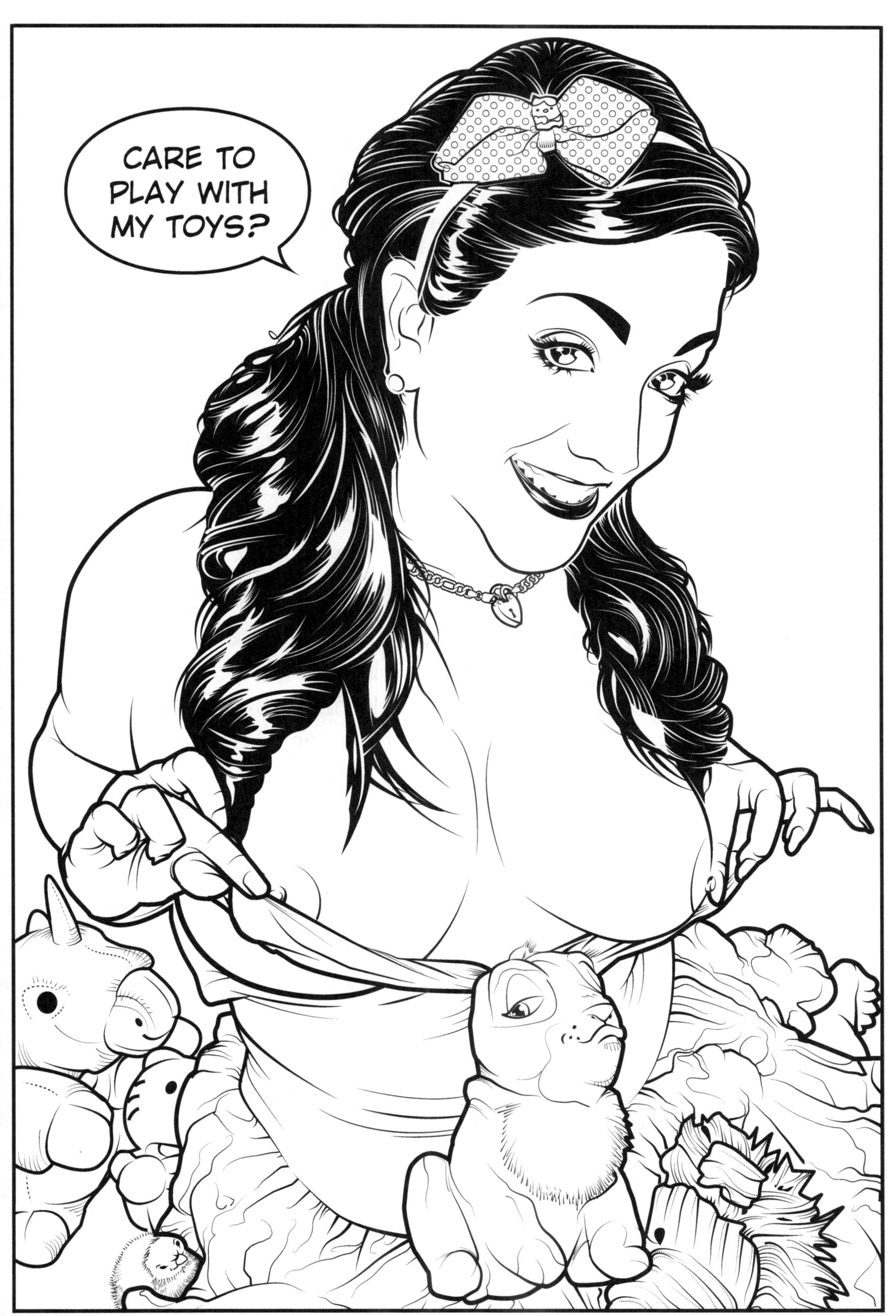
CARE TO PLAY WITH MY TOYS?

Unfortunately, it has been awhile since I have had the chance to visit FreakyMar5. I hope once I make the print deadline I have for this coloring book that I'll be able to change that. She is really a great person to have hanging around.

Hanging Around

Model: Freakymar5

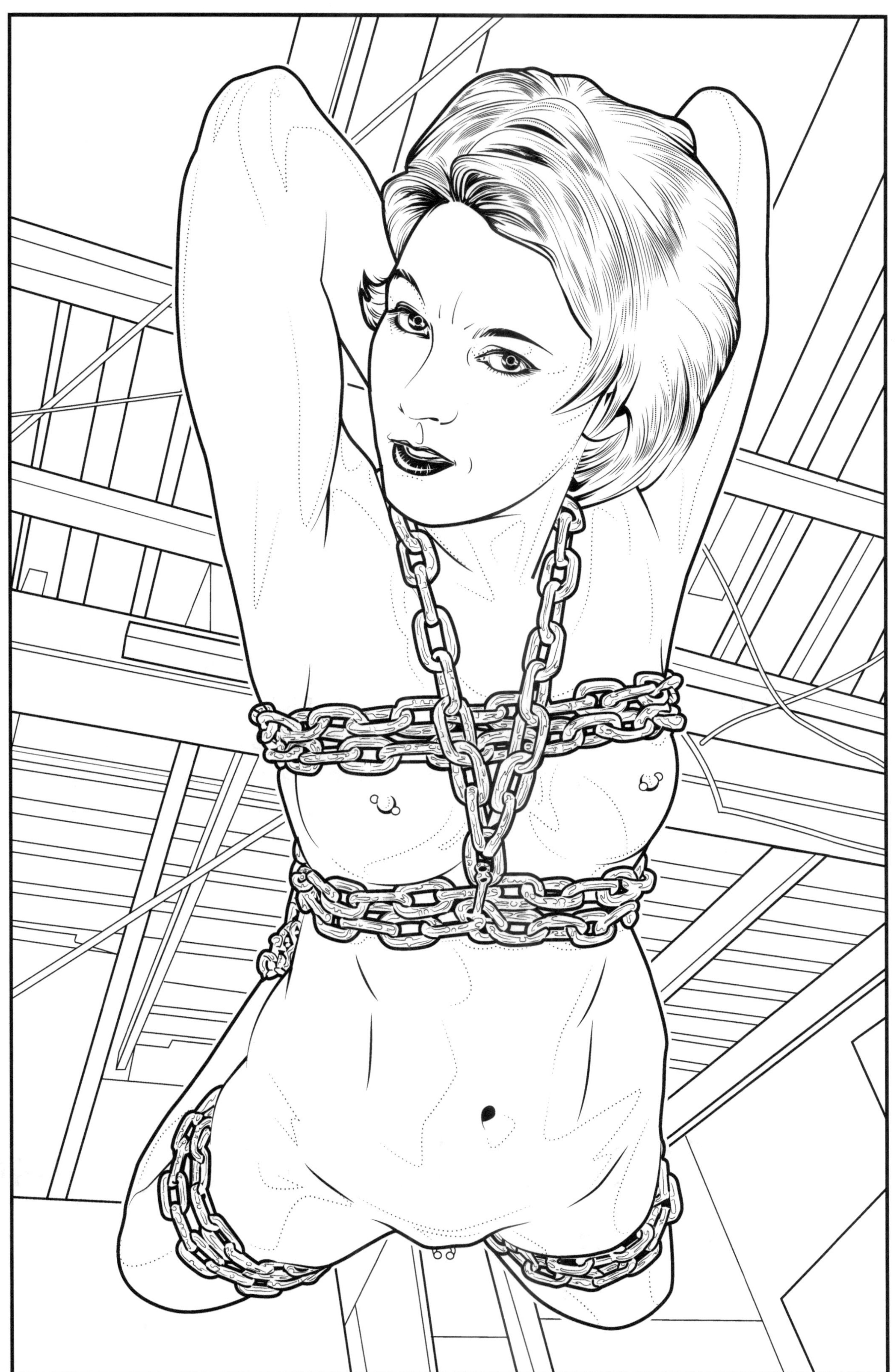

I have always wanted to do an Art Nouveau illustration for this book, since that is the period of art I really enjoy. Art Nouveau is way harder than it looks, though. There is a lot of interplay between the negative space and the graphic elements you use that all need to be considered. Despite the difficulties, I'm sure I will be coming back to this style again.

Kara Catonic in Art Nouveau

Model: Kara Catonic

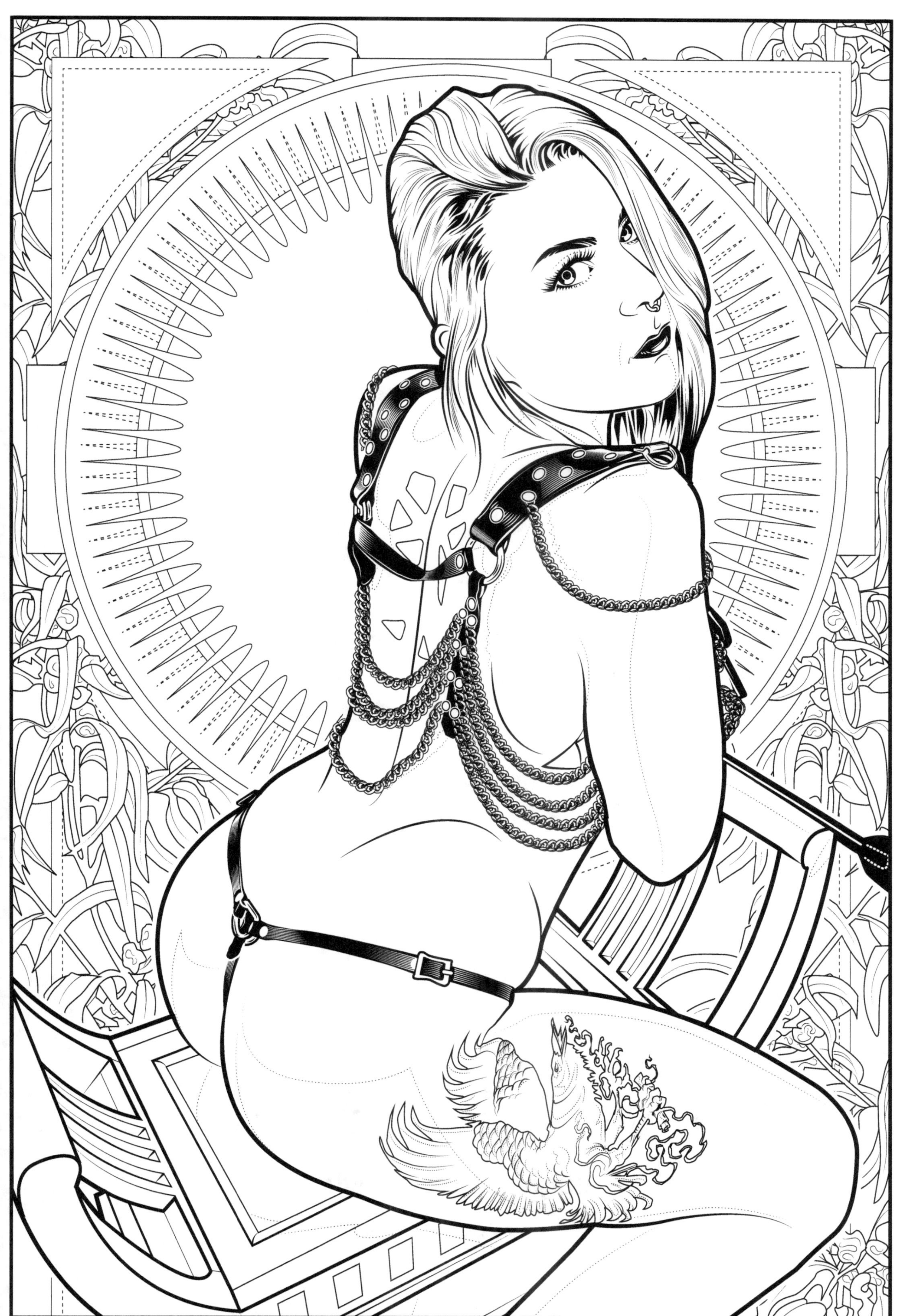

This was my first completed coloring book illustration of 2015. I took it as a good sign.

Barb Wire Saint

Model: Basia, Rope Rigging: CorruptMorals

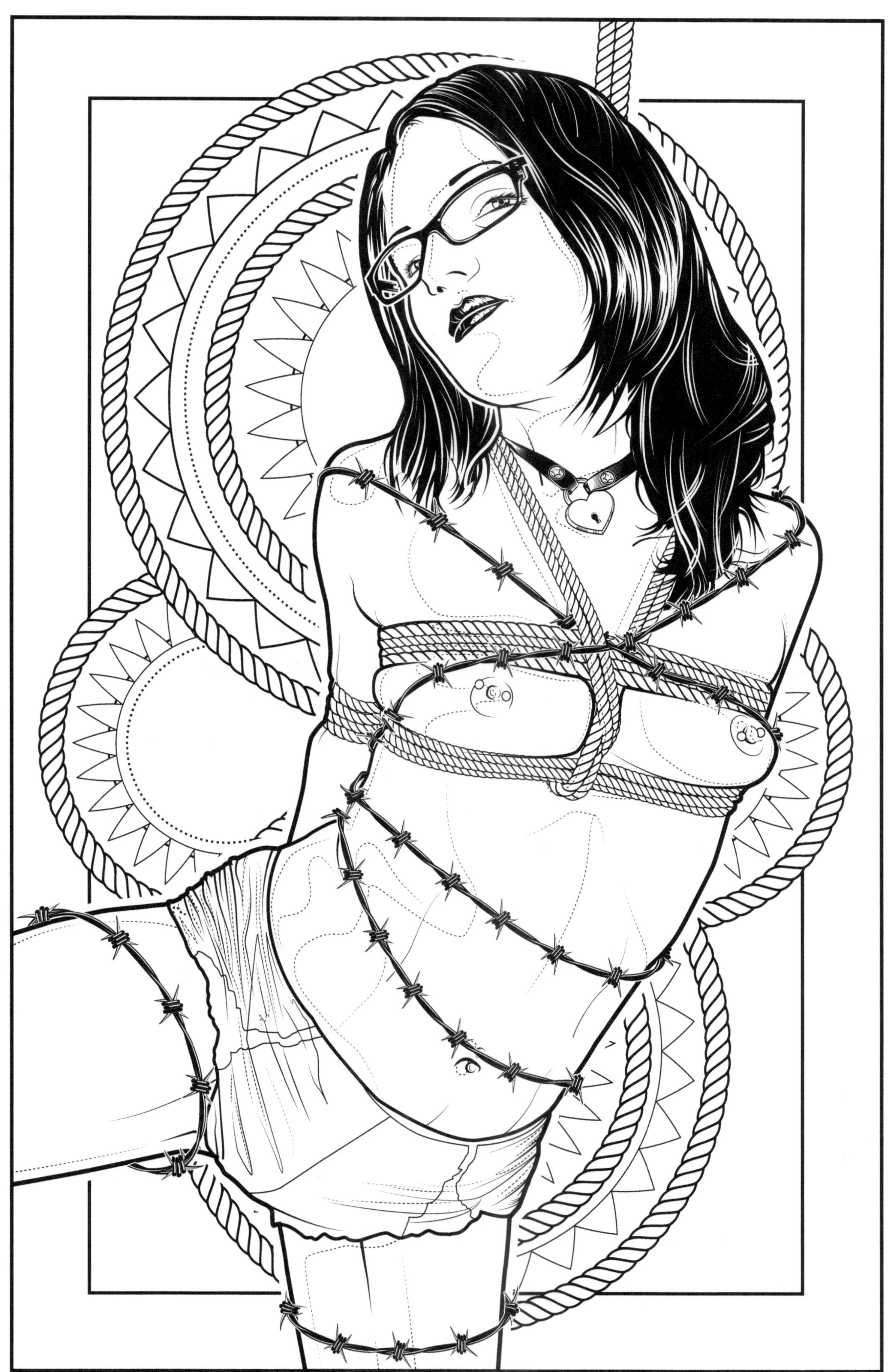

Back when I was in art school majoring in illustration, I had to take a semester-long course drawing nothing but heads and hands. Except for the face, the hands are the most expressive parts of the body. We spent hours learning to draw them. It is nice to know that all that time in the basement studio of the Powell Street building paid off.

Holding Hands

Models: Raven Le Faye & Chelsea Christian

Latex Dresses by Lust Designs

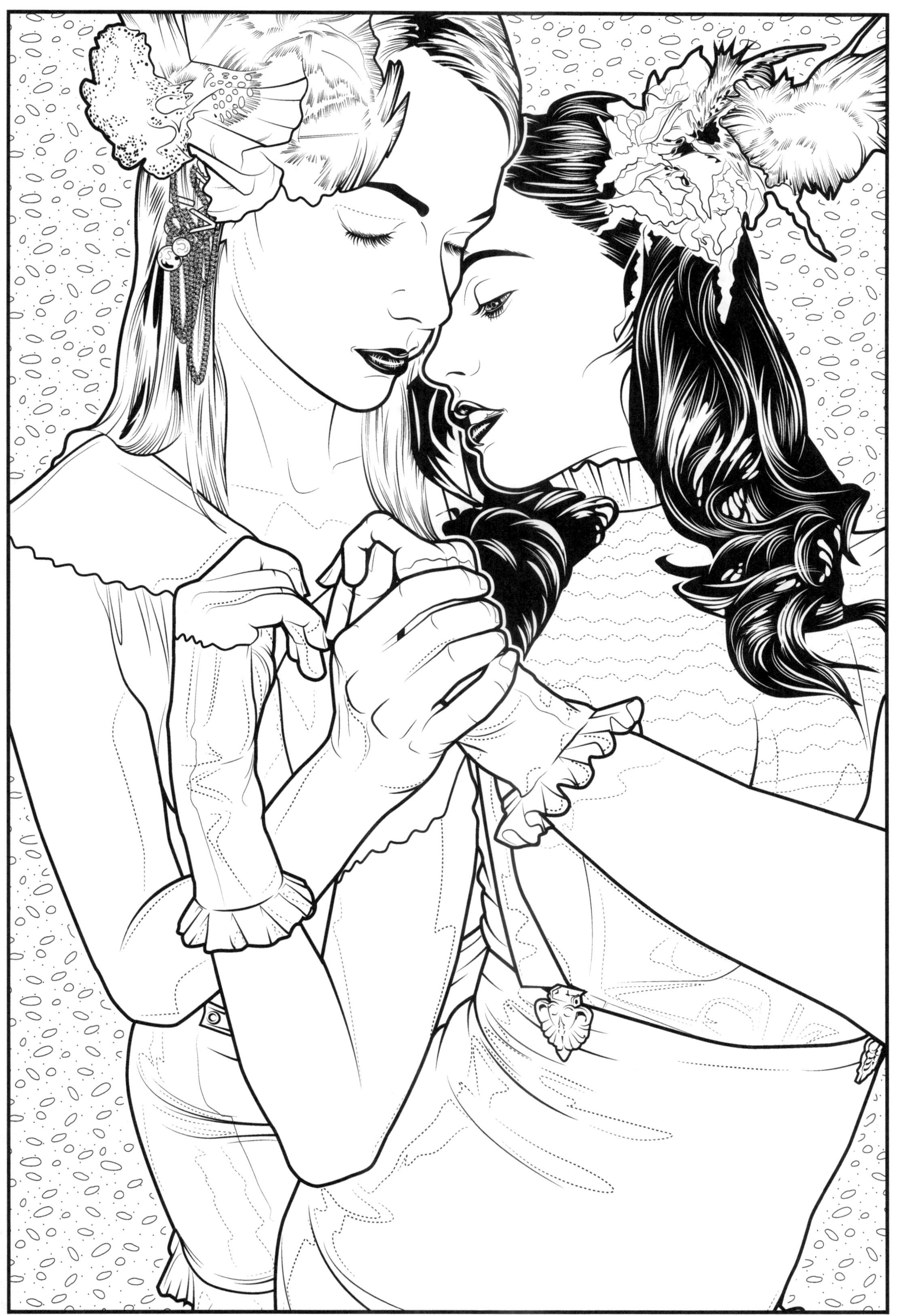

How can anyone say no to such a pretty face?

Kitty Begging

Models: Aurora and Kara Catonic, Rigger: Roboticized

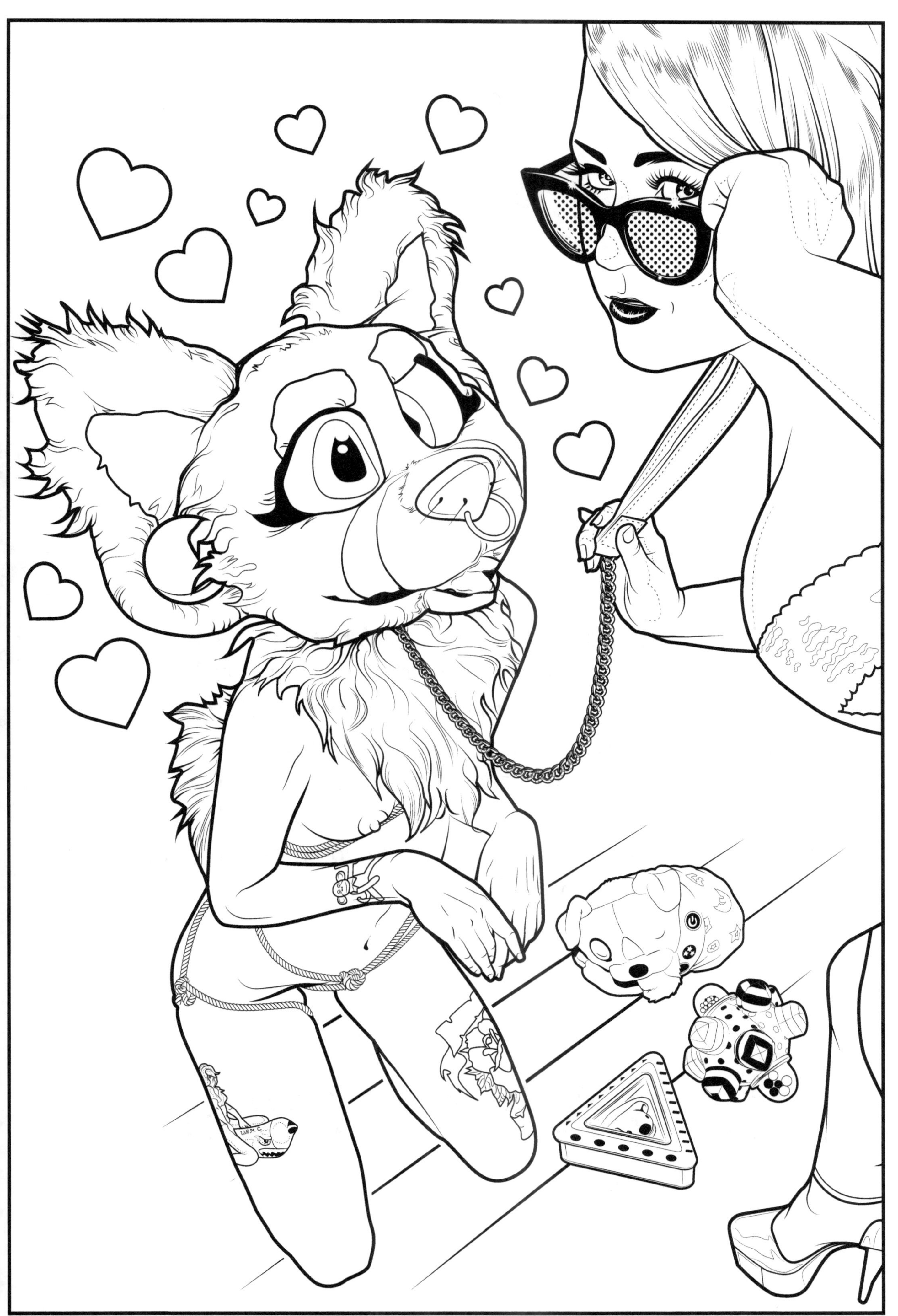

Here's another illustration of Daisy on Jim Higgin's naked motorcycle. According to Jim, a "naked" motorcycle refers to the lack of bodywork shielding you from the wind, so you are riding exposed. Basically, it's used for the motorcycle equivalent of drag racing, i.e., seeing how fast you can go in a straight line. I suspect that Daisy's shapely butt sticking out like that would slow the bike down with wind resistance, but I think we can live with that.

Naked Motorcycle

Model: Daisy Night

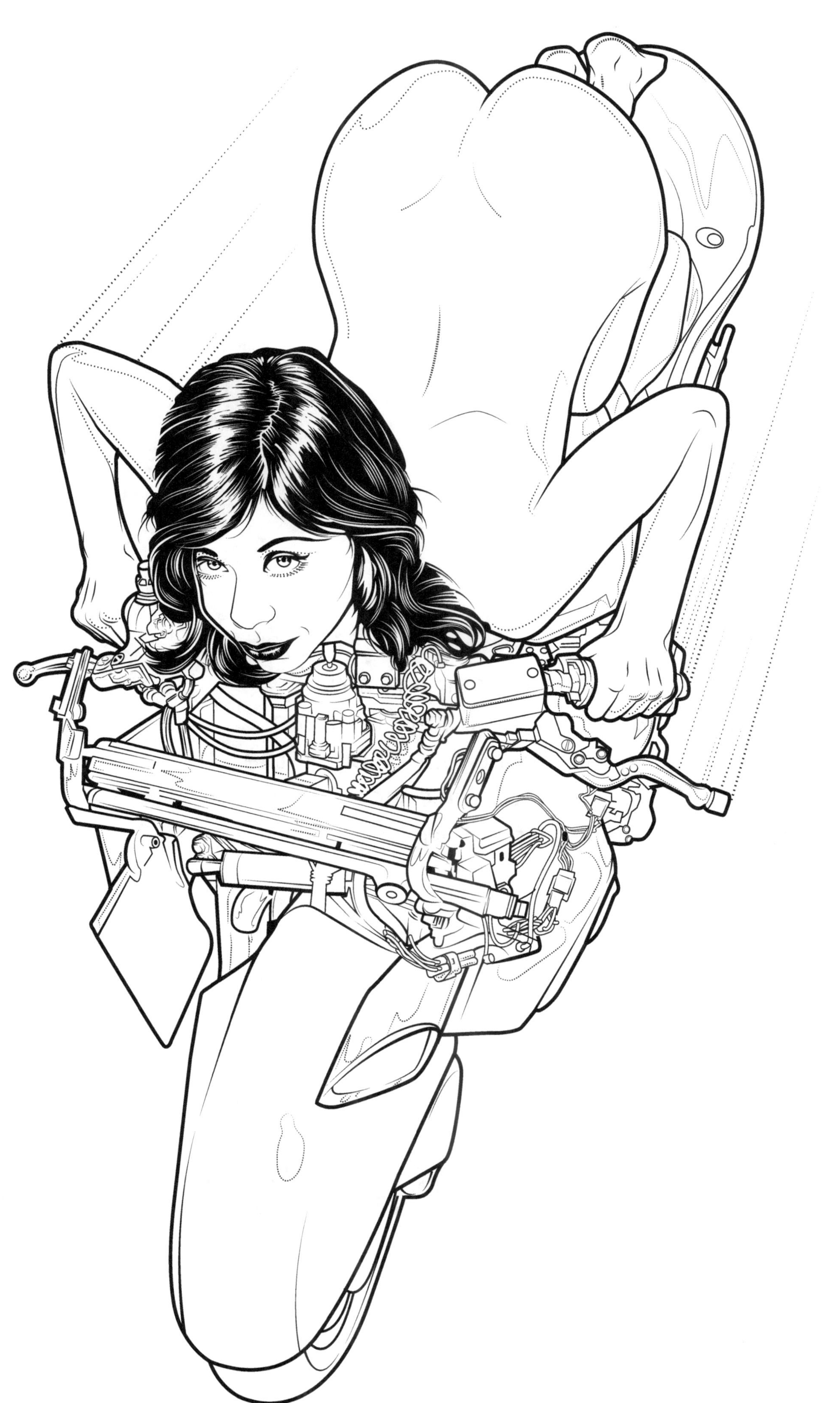

A friend of mine told me when she saw this picture that she wanted to yell, "That's crochet!" That gave me the idea to put in the knitting project by his feet. Kink comes in all sizes, shapes and colors of yarn.

Naughty Knitter

Location: Folsom Street Fair

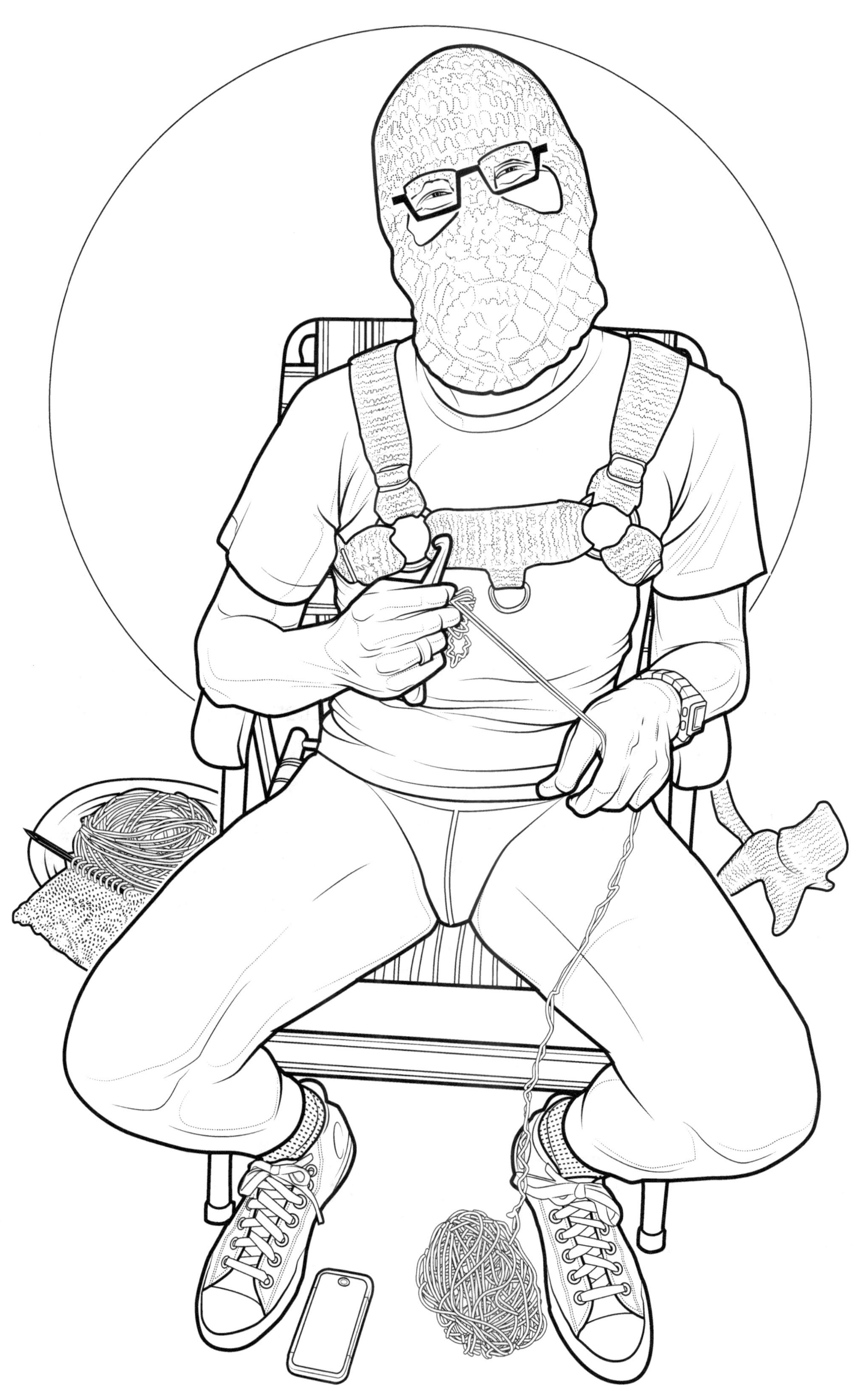

Despite the fact that she had multiple tattoos on her body, and a large one on her chest, Basia was reluctant to do any needle play on her boobies.

Note: I realize that I drew bare hands holding the needle. This is just artistic license. The truth is that you should NEVER needle top someone without wearing gloves, and you should not play with someone that doesn't wear them.

Needle Virgin

Model: Basia

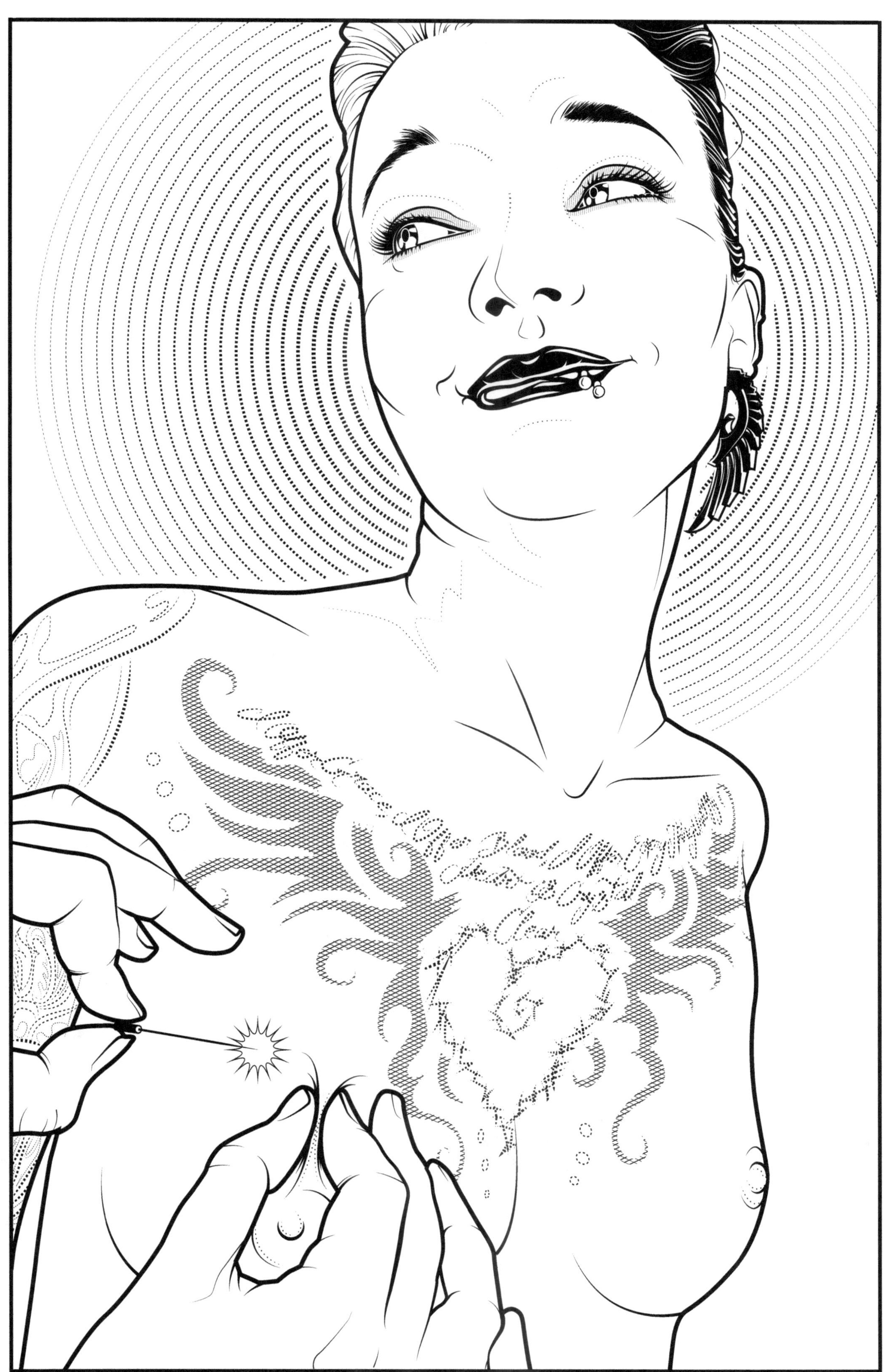

For a good time, call...

Party Time

Model: Tia Leigh

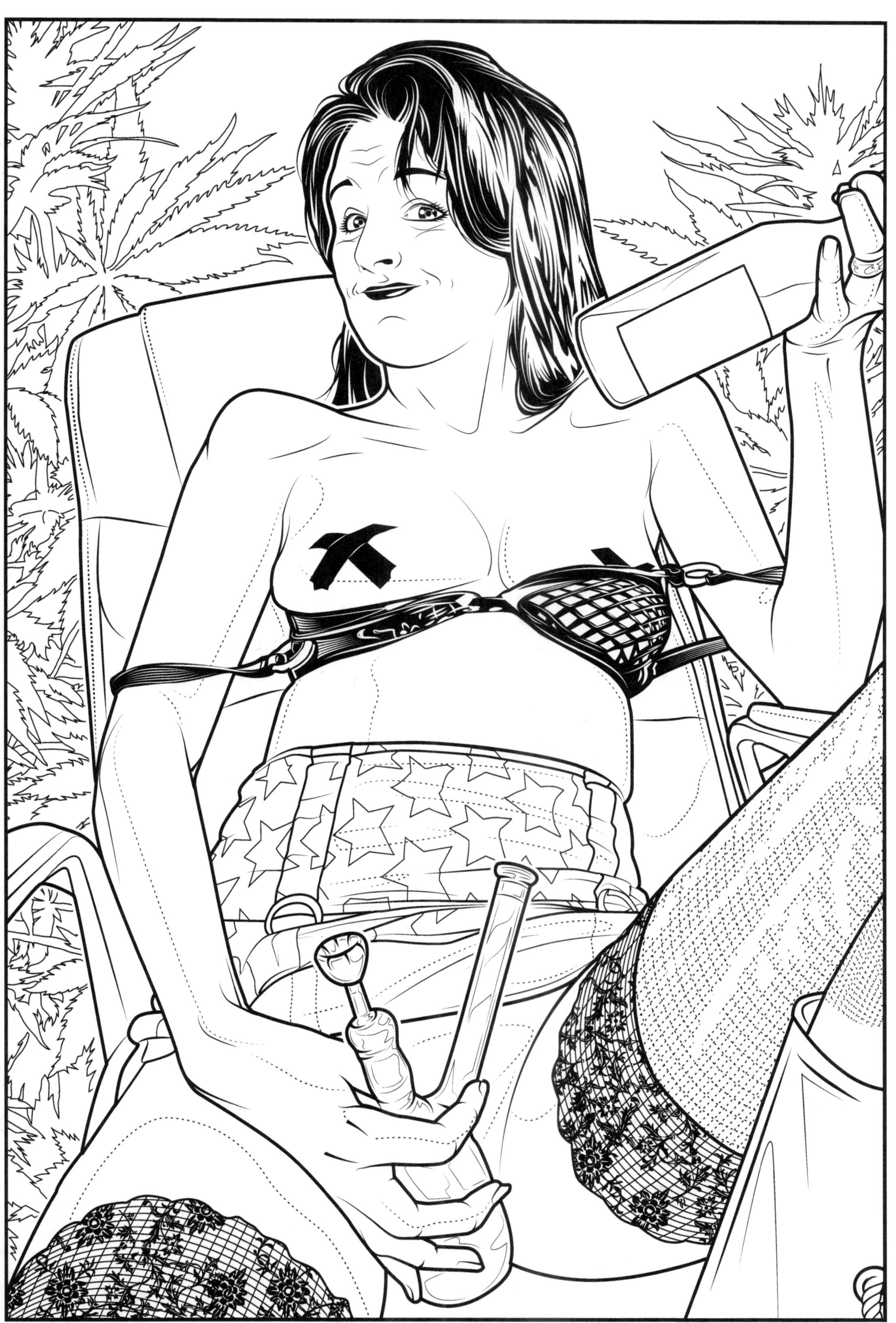

Many people like to go to Folsom Street Fair to see the naked people walking around, but I like to go and see the interesting outfits. Many kinksters spend hundreds of dollars on these outfits, and they put in hours and hours of work creating them. Ironically, this may be the only time of year when many of these outfits actually see daylight.

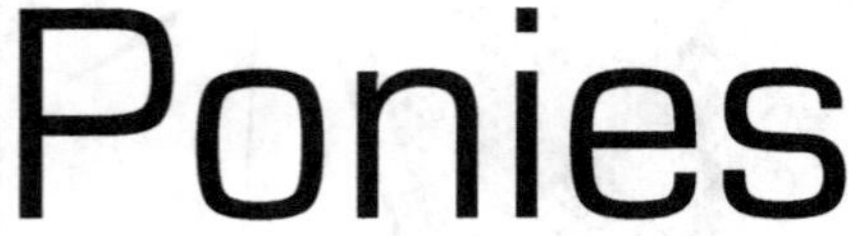

Ponies

Model: The Twins

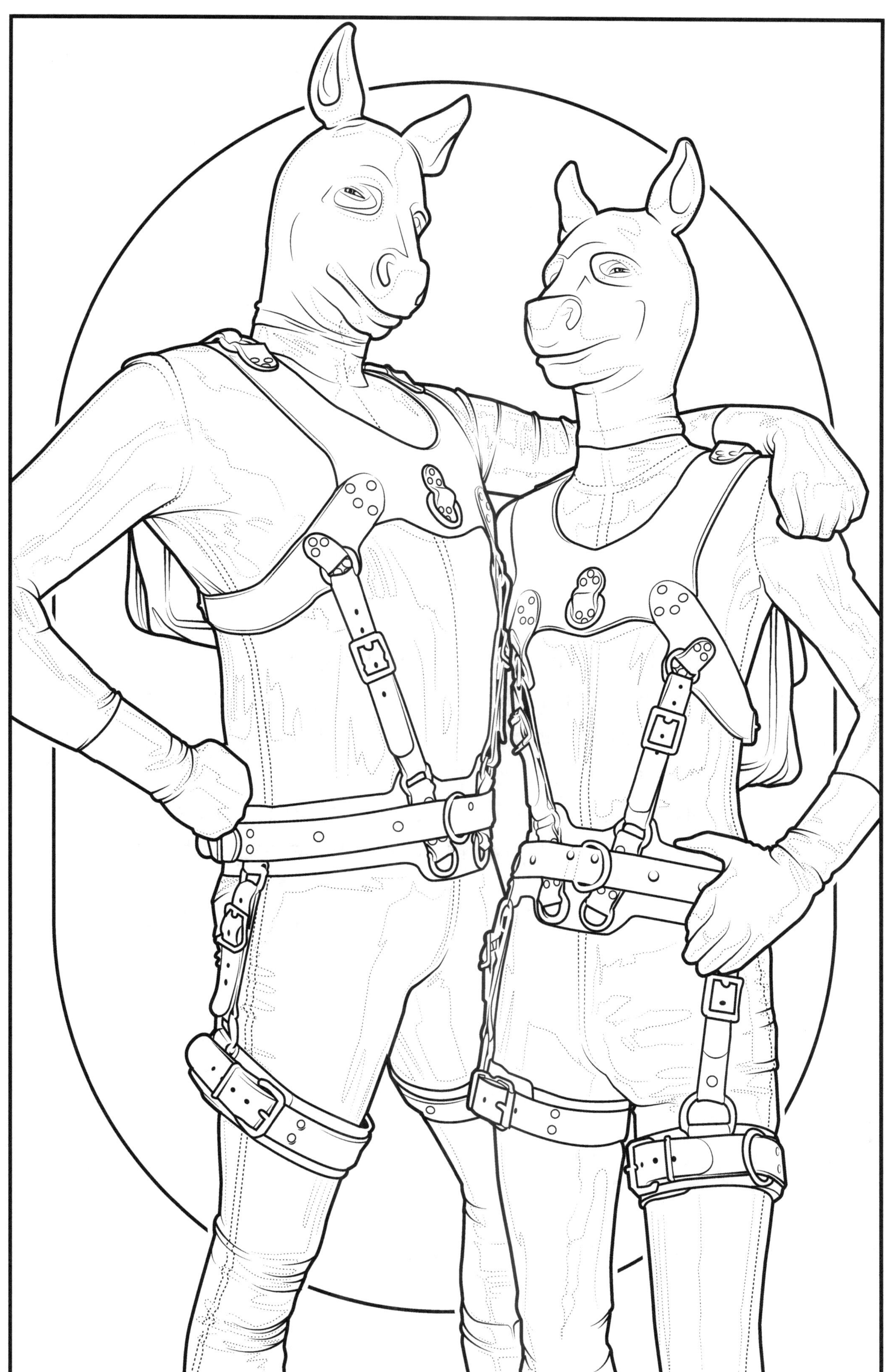

The other thing I like about the Folsom Street Fair is watching the live demos performed on stages all around the fair. But let's face it, once you let somebody tie up your cock and balls in rope, you pretty much have a good idea of what is coming. Nevertheless, I have always enjoyed the look of absolute surrender on the main figure in this picture.

Rope Guy

Location: Folsom Street Fair 2013

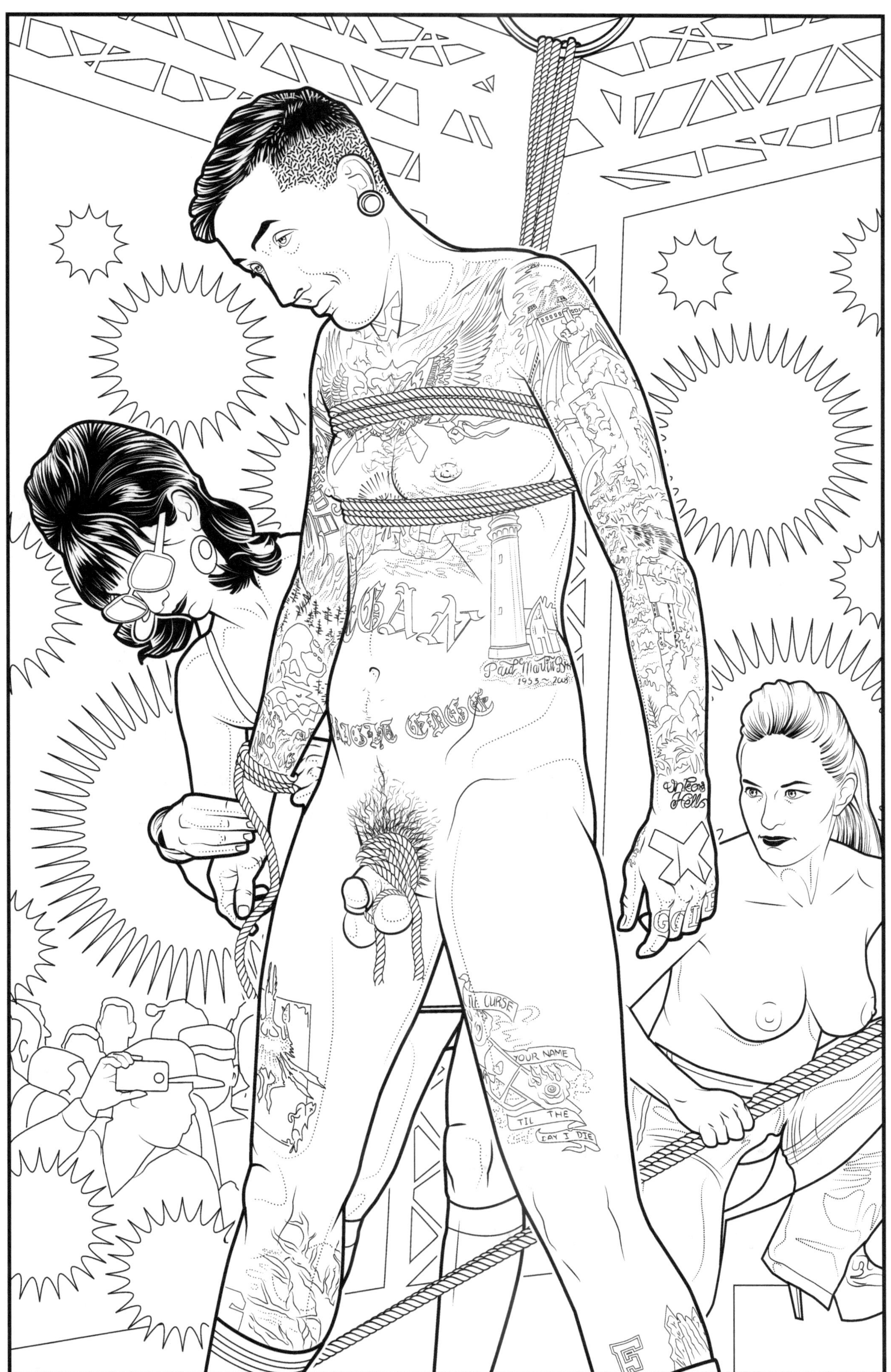
1953 ~ 2008
YOUR NAME
TIL THE
DAY I DIE

Promethea told me once how one of the things on her "bucket list" was to be in one of my Kinky Coloring Books. Though I'm not in any hurry to see her kick-off just yet, I'm glad I'll be able to make her wish come true. I love how utterly decadent she looks in this pose. It fits, since working with her was a satisfying experience.

Promethea

Models: Promethea and Pervette

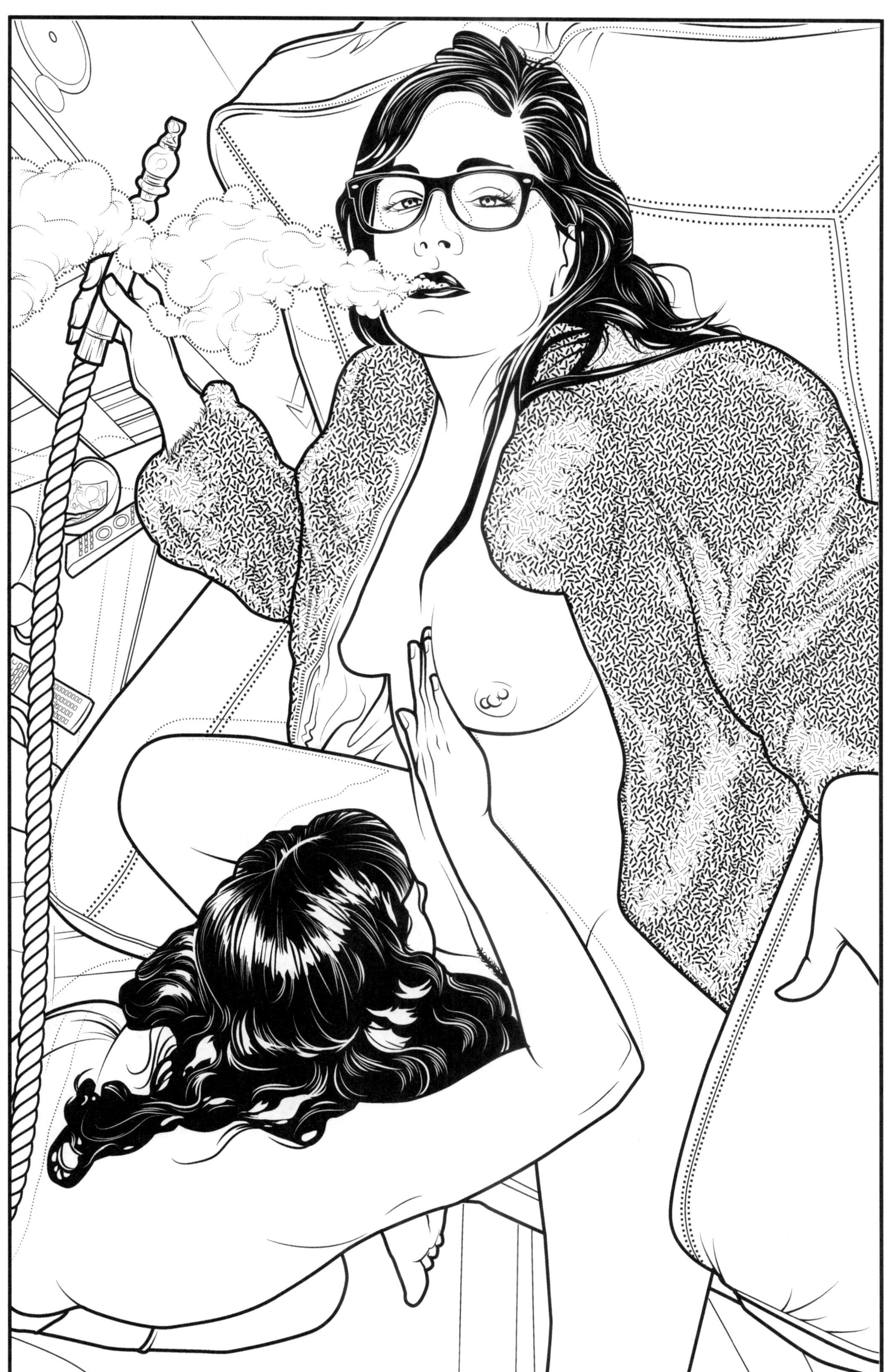

At one point, I kept thinking this image needed more stuff, but whatever I added seemed to detract from it. So finally I just decided to stop and call it done. Making images more complex doesn't always make them better.

Little Chelsea

Model: Chelsea Christian, Latex dress by Lust Designs

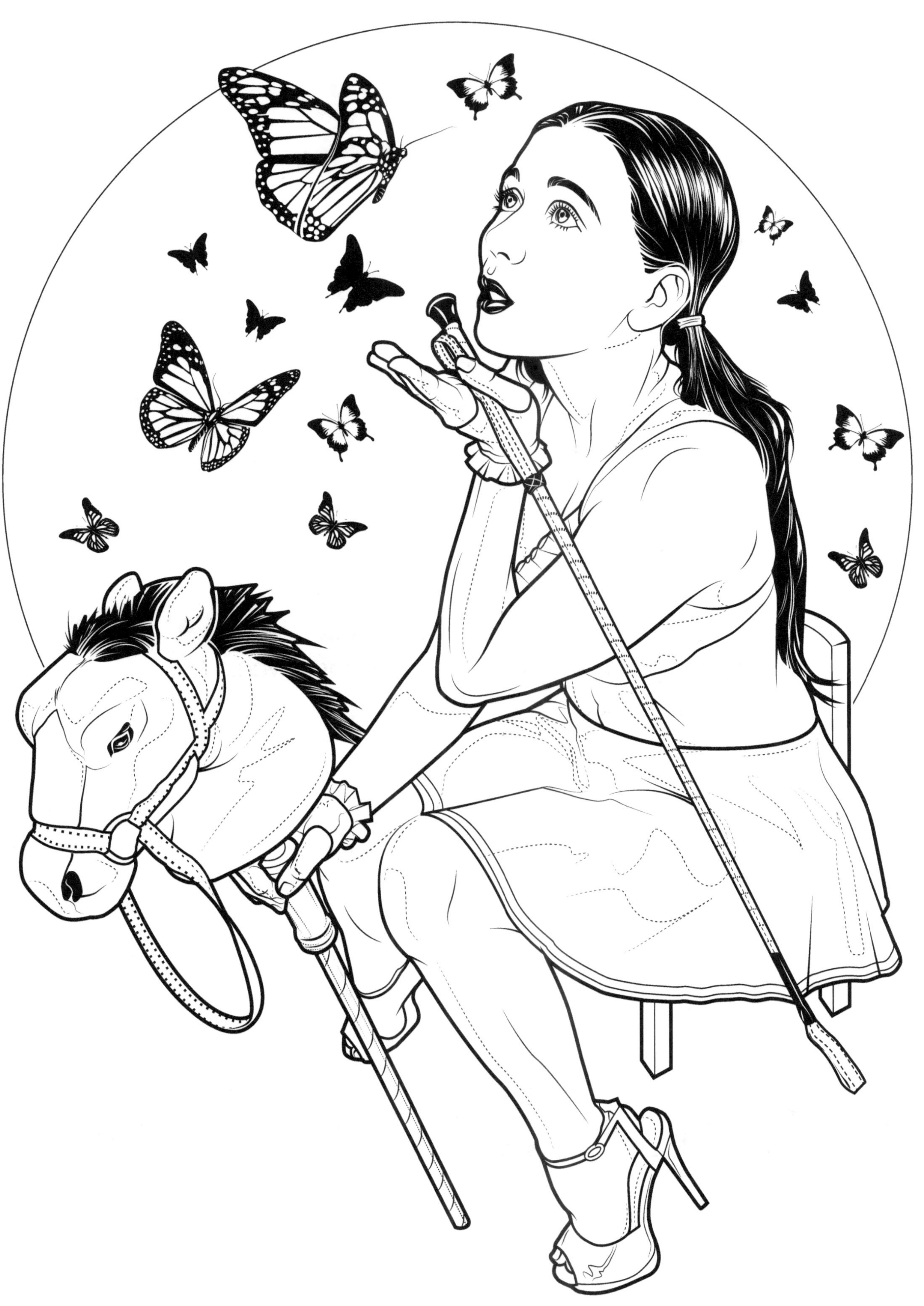

If some guy were to ever say, "Hey bitch, make me a sandwich," this is what I imagine Tia's response would be to that particular request.

The Sandwich Maker

Model: Tia Leigh

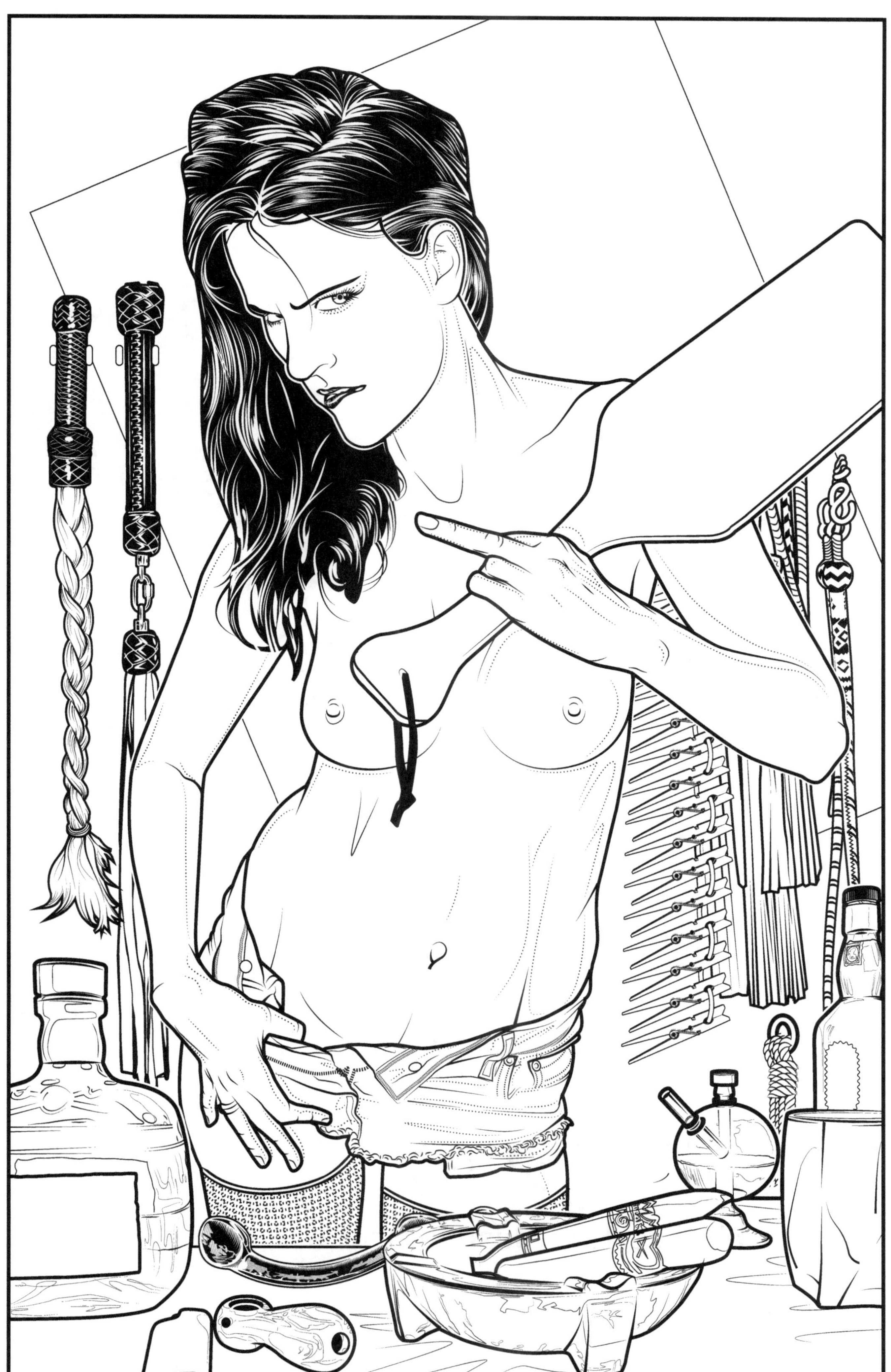

I thought Justina did an awesome job on Libby's hair the day of our photo shoot. I always have fun drawing it when it is time to illustrate.

Submissive

Model: Libby Loo, Hair: Justina Downs

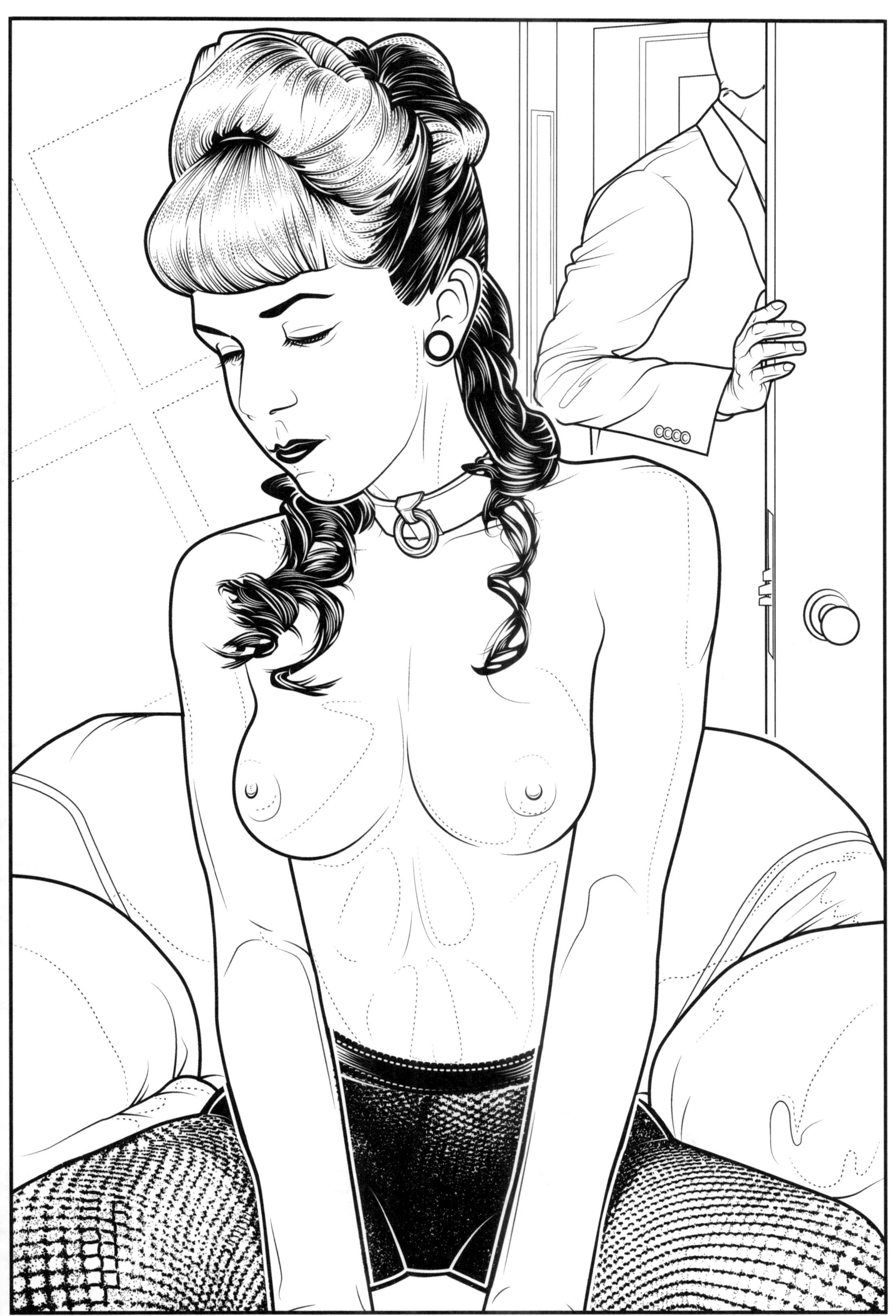

Women are like flames of a fire. Even though you know you can get burned, you are still drawn in by the heat.

Temptress

Model: Raven Le Faye, Rope Rigging: CorruptMorals

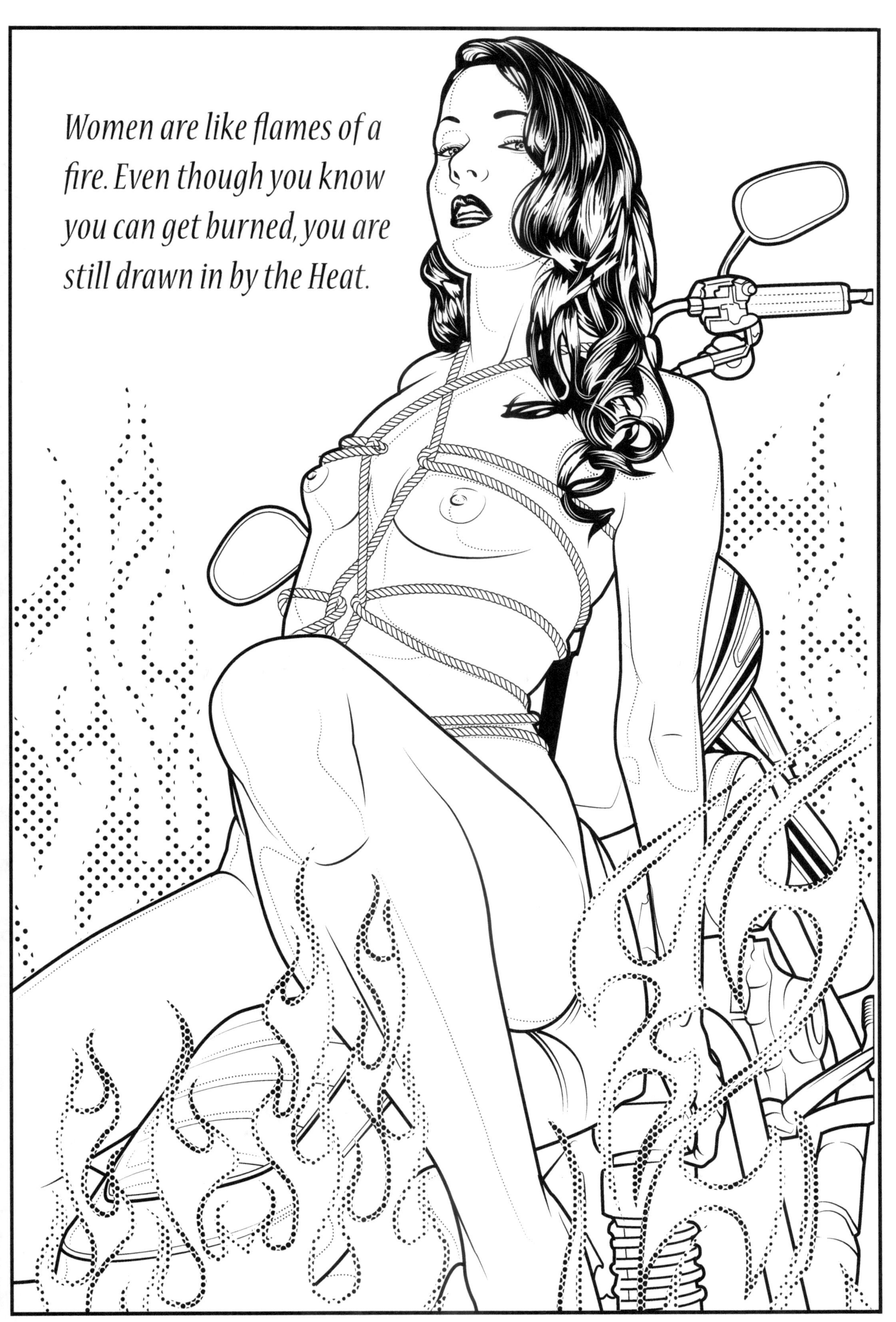
Women are like flames of a fire. Even though you know you can get burned, you are still drawn in by the Heat.

Aurora actually has this tattoo across her chest. It probably hurt more than a single “Ow” can express.

The Raven Tattoo

Models: Aurora and Kara Catonic

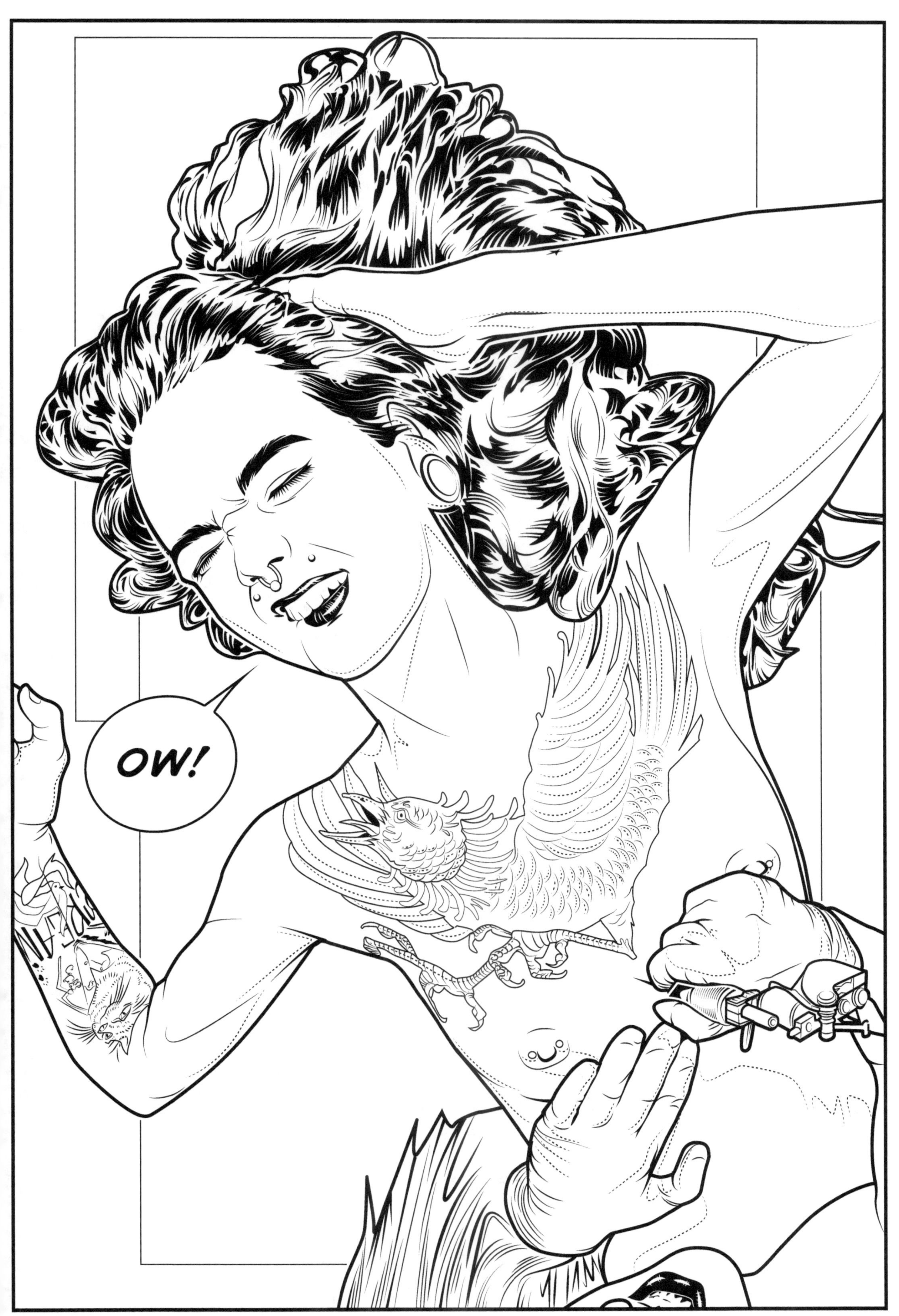
OW!

Because Mommy would never hurt you...right?

Trust Mommy

Models: Promethea and Pervette

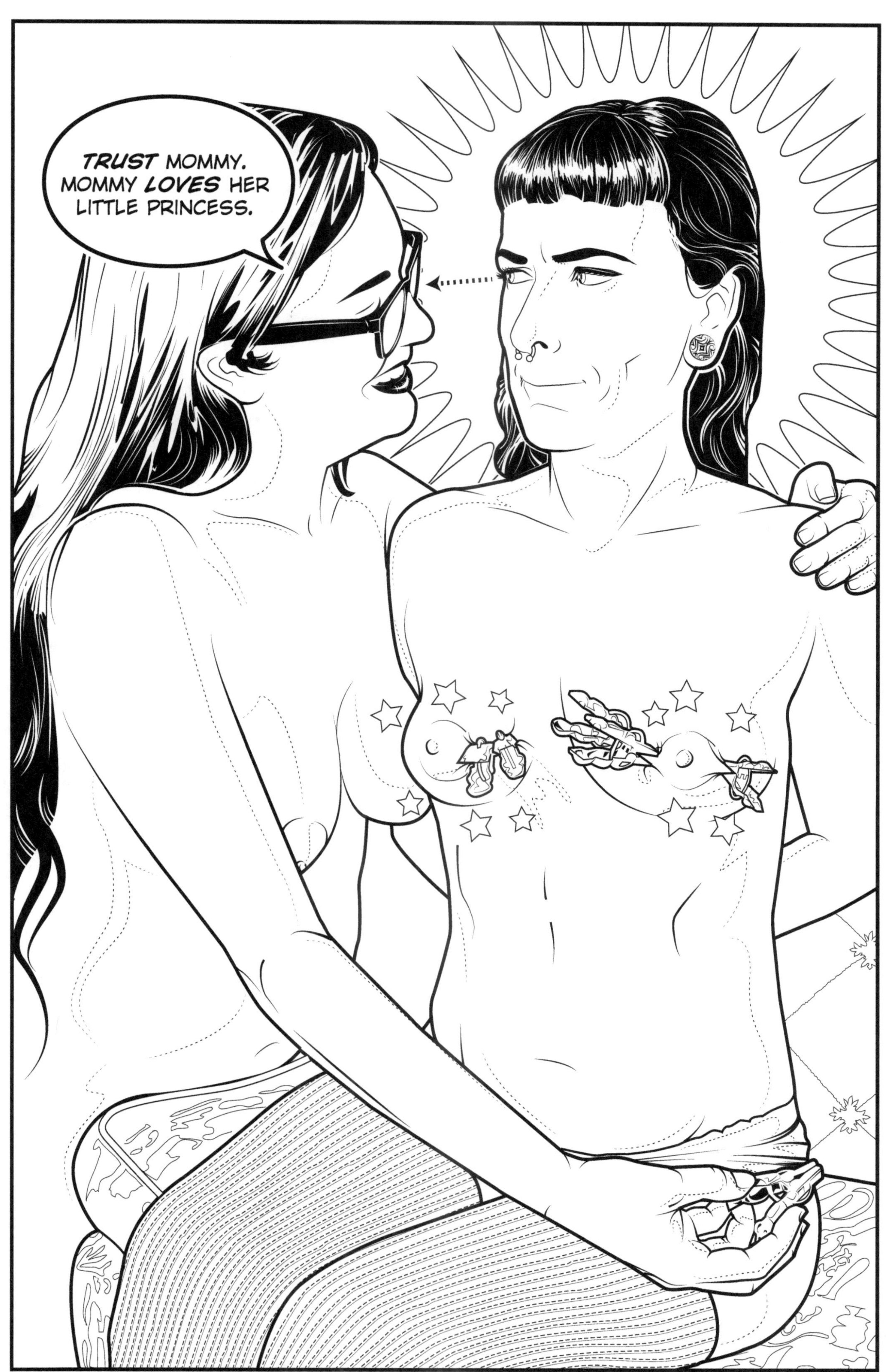
TRUST MOMMY. MOMMY LOVES HER LITTLE PRINCESS.

www.ingramcontent.com/pod-product-compliance
Lightning Source LLC
LaVergne TN
LVHW081151110826
845149LV00008B/1618
* 9 7 8 0 9 8 5 8 9 9 9 3 6 *